Siren Ménage E

The *story behind The Lost Collection

During recent excavations in several abandoned western U.S. mining towns, a Siren editor/archaeology enthusiast discovered crates of old, tattered diaries and journals buried and lost for more than 100 years.

Hot passion and daring romance was alive and well among the intrepid women of the Old West. Siren Publishing invited a few of our most distinguished bestselling authors to take on new pseudonyms and use their imaginations to bring to life some of the love stories of the Old West.

Once Siren releases the 50th book in The Lost Collection, we will reveal the identity of some of these authors.

* a fictional account

Lana Dare

BEAUMONTS' BRAND

Ménage Everlasting

© SIRENpublishing.com

BEAUMONTS' BRAND

The Lost Collection

Lana Dare

MENAGE EVERLASTING

Siren Publishing, Inc.
www.SirenPublishing.com

BEAUMONTS' BRAND

LANA DARE
Copyright © 2010

Chapter One

Victoria Fowler stilled. Coming to her feet, she turned, listening as the sound of approaching riders got louder with each passing second.

They were coming back!

She looked around frantically for the best place to hide. Eyeing her collection of weapons, she made a hasty decision. She kept the large knife strapped to her belt and dropped Frank's knife into her boot. Buck's knife, the one that he'd worn strapped to his own belt, would be too big to fit comfortably in her other boot, so she carried it with her.

She hadn't been able to find Will's knife and James's had been broken. Wishing for the hundredth time their guns hadn't been taken, she scrambled up the slope for cover.

The ungodly noise kept growing and her heart raced as she thought of the possibilities. Did they realize that there had been five horses but only four riders? Did they go through the saddlebags, find her clothing and decide to come back?

Scrambling up the ridge to an outcropping of boulders, she fought the waves of dizziness that nearly took her to her knees. She hadn't eaten in two days and her body grew weaker with each passing hour. She'd hoped to find something among the destruction the men and the coyotes left behind, but the only thing she found had been the knives and her brothers' remains.

Fighting nausea and dizziness, she raced up the hill, slipping on several loose stones. Once she finally managed to get behind the rocks, she stopped and listened, trying to quiet her breathing. The noise got louder and closer, far too loud to be just a few riders. Could it be soldiers? They'd run across many soldiers along the way, some not even knowing the aggression had ended.

Would she be rescued?

As the noise grew even louder, she heard raised voices and whistles. Peeking around the rocks, she blinked when she saw what looked like hundreds of cows.

Cows? Why would there be cows out here?

A horse came into view, the rider wearing a kerchief over his mouth and nose, hiding his face. Holy juniper. She'd never seen a man that big before. When his gaze slid in her direction, she hurriedly ducked back behind the rock.

The only reason for a man to cover his face that way would be if he were a bandit. But why would he have it covered out here in the middle of nowhere?

The cows kept coming and she blinked, wondering if she was seeing things. She peeked again to see another man, surprised to see he looked every bit as large as the first. The second paused next to the first and motioned to several other riders, who quickly rode ahead.

Both men wore chaps and cowboy hats, not the uniforms she'd hoped for.

They slowed and herded the cows into a ravine not far from where she hid. The two big men, along with several others, got off of their horses in the clearing as even more riders diverted the cows.

Panicked now by the sheer number of men, she slowly worked her way around to another large rock, putting a little more distance between her and them. With a sinking heart, she watched as a wagon brought up the rear and stopped in the clearing.

The two big men appeared to be in charge, barking out orders to the others. With their faces now uncovered, they walked over to the hole she'd been digging and paused when they saw the remains of her brothers.

Tears slid down her cheeks as she watched them get a shovel from the wagon and finish the job she'd been unable to complete. Silently thanking them, she sent up a quick prayer for her brothers' souls.

Some of the men set up camp, gathering firewood and coming to the pond to fill pots with water. Others stayed with the horses, leading them to the pond for a drink while still more men stayed with the cows.

She tried to count them, but they moved around too much for her to keep track. The two who appeared to be in charge conferred with a grizzly older man, all three scanning the surrounding area the entire time. She moved around the rock to look out from the other side, staying low so they couldn't spot her.

The smell of food cooking made her stomach growl and weakened her even more. The two larger men kept looking at the ground as though trying to follow a trail, but with all the prints on the ground, she hoped they wouldn't be able to follow hers.

Approaching the small pond, they scanned the area, forcing her to duck down again. Lying on her belly, she looked through the tall brush down to where the two men studied the footprints around the pond. The way they kept looking at the ground, occasionally kneeling down to touch something, and then lifting their gazes to the rocks where she hid scared the bejesus out of her. Could they track her?

She would love to go down there and ask for help, but she didn't yet know if she should trust them. Her life depended on her not making a bad decision. Staying hidden seemed the best option for now. Checking that her knife still remained in her belt, she hunkered down to wait, trying to ignore the tantalizing smells that drifted to her.

She would wait until they all fell asleep. Perhaps then she could steal some food.

* * * *

Ben Beaumont tossed the dregs of his coffee into a bush, his gaze touching on each of his men before scanning the surrounding area again. Three more days and he'd be home. For the fourth time in as many years, he and his brother, Wade, made the long cattle drive from Texas to Montana. This would be their last.

Several of the ranch hands made claims on their behalf. Combined they finally had more than ten thousand acres and enough cattle to build their ranch on. He wished their folks could have seen it.

With beef prices up North rising and the large amount of newcomers, he and Wade managed to build something grand. With this additional cattle, they would do even better.

He loved his home, and he hated being away from it. Their foreman, Jeb Smith, handled everything well enough while they were gone, but Ben still hated not being there. There would be a million and one things that needed his attention when he got back.

He had a good life, a life he and his brother worked hard for. They had everything they'd ever wanted.

Except a good woman.

Once he and Wade got home and caught up on whatever they'd missed in the last several months, Ben wanted to take a wife. The decision was made before they'd left and these past few months made him even more determined.

Almost thirty years old, he figured he should settle down. Winter came early in Montana, and his bed got damned cold. He couldn't imagine any of the working girls in town being happy on the ranch, but with the lack of women around, he couldn't afford to be choosy. Maybe he would send for one of those mail order brides he'd heard about.

Hell, he didn't have time to think about that now.

His gaze swept the ravine where the cattle were herded for the night. The first watch would be about over, and it would be time for his. He should have gotten some sleep by now, but he'd been too edgy to settle.

They'd found the bodies of four men, or what was left of them, not far from where he stood now, along with coyote tracks. He had a hard time believing that coyotes could attack four grown men without the men killing at least one of them. Had the men been asleep? Completely unarmed?

No man went around unarmed. The whole thing just didn't make sense.

It made him uneasy, and he couldn't wait to move on.

"What the hell's wrong with you? You're as restless as a cat in a room full of rockers."

Ben looked over at his brother. "No sign of trouble?"

Wade shrugged as he shook out his bedroll. "No. Nothing. Red and I took another look around. It looks like they came from the east. Five horses, one ridin' light."

"Damn. Only four bodies, or what was left of them after the coyotes got done with 'em. I hope the other wasn't a woman or a kid that they took with 'em."

"Woulda been better off dead."

"Yeah. How the hell did coyotes get 'em?"

Wade scrubbed a hand over his face. "Don't seem possible, does it? Ben, you'd better get some shut eye. You're on watch soon."

Ben nodded and lay down on his bedroll, listening to Shorty snore. Lying there staring at the stars, he sent up a quick prayer for the one who'd survived. Propping his hat over his eyes, he tried to settle down to sleep.

* * * *

Ben came awake in an instant, his gun already in his hand. His hat hid most of his face as he saw the small figure work his way clumsily to the chuck wagon. Aware of Wade's alertness beside him, he remained silent as he watched the figure look around nervously while stumbling forward.

Wearing pants rolled up several times and a shirt that hung down to his knees, the figure looked like a boy in his daddy's clothes. Moving almost, but not quite silently, he continued to make his way closer and closer to the wagon, staggering like a drunk. The fire burned too low to see the boy's face clearly. With the kid's hat pulled so low, Ben wondered if he could even see. Once the boy got close enough to the wagon, he held on as though for support, and it took him three tries before he made it inside.

Ben waved back the hands that stood when he did, putting a finger to his lips as he and Wade moved forward. Tucking his gun away, he approached from one side while Wade approached from the other. Aware of his men moving in behind him, he waved them back, not wanting anyone to accidentally shoot the kid.

Wondering if this kid had anything to do with the four dead men, he shot a glance at his brother and nodded. Wade pointed his gun skyward and reached up with his free hand to grab the kid's ankles, pulling him from the wagon.

The feminine squeal shocked the hell out of him as the small figure fell to the ground with a thud, drawing a knife that Wade quickly grabbed away.

Kneeling and holding on to her arm, Ben glanced over his shoulder. "Red, bring me a lantern."

The small figure began thrashing. "Let me go. I didn't do anything."

He and Wade looked at each other in surprise. It *was* a female, one who sounded weak and breathless. He let go, not wanting to add to her obvious fear.

She staggered to her feet, backing away. Her hat fell off and a long, blonde braid now hung down her back. "Please don't hurt me. I'll go away. I didn't steal anything, I swear. I just wanted some food."

Red came running with a lantern and held it up, allowing them to get a good look at her.

John Dodge laughed, the sound of it making Ben clench his jaw. "Well, looky what we got here."

Ben heard several gasps from behind him as the men realized it was a woman, one with a dirty, sunburned face. "We won't hurt you. Were you with those men we found earlier?"

When her legs buckled, Wade caught her before she could hit the ground again. "Yes. My brothers. Put me down. Don't touch me."

Wade ignored her protests, lifting her in his arms.

Ben took the lantern from Red. "Shorty, go get some water." He followed as Wade carried her to his bedroll.

Wade laid her down gently, despite her weak struggles. "How long have you been hiding here?"

Her eyes, wet with tears, looked bluer than any Ben had ever seen. The fear in them kept him from reaching for her as he knelt down beside her.

She kept looking from him to Wade, her eyes wide. "Since yesterday. I just wanted some food. I haven't eaten since yesterday morning. I wasn't going to steal anything else. I swear."

Wade, kneeling on her other side, lowered his voice, speaking to her as he would a frightened animal. "Don't be afraid. Can you sit up?"

Ben held out a hand in case she needed help, but she cringed and backed away.

Accepting the pan from Shorty, Wade took off his kerchief and poured water on it. "She looks like she's got sunstroke. I'll bet she's got a fever. Look at her eyes."

Shorty grabbed the lantern to hold it up so the men could take care of her. "She's just a little thing. She been out here two days by herself? Lucky the coyotes didn't git her."

Ben poured more water on the kerchief Wade held out, shooting Shorty a dirty look. "Hobble your lip, Shorty." Wade gently wiped her face and neck. With the dirt wiped away, her features became clearer. She looked young, but not as young as he'd first thought. Her full breasts rose and fell with each breath. No, she wasn't a child.

Cookie hurried over with a few leftover biscuits, the gruff older man pushing his way through the others. "Here. Coupla these ought to hold her 'til breakfast."

Ben broke a biscuit in half and handed it to her, knowing she would eat it too fast. When she did, he made her drink a little water before handing her the other half. He did the same thing with the second and the third, not giving her too much at once and making her wash it down before giving her any more. On the third she finally slowed down, watching them all warily.

It didn't take long before her eyes began to droop. Each time they did, she forced them open but it took longer and longer. After the last two days, she had to be tuckered out. He helped her lie back as Wade continued to tend to her. Finally her eyes closed and stayed that way.

Wade continued to bathe her face and neck with cool water. "I'll watch over her while you're on watch. She's as weak as a newborn kitten."

Shorty shook his head. "She's been hidin' here all day, and we didn't find her."

Shrugging, Red turned away. "Didn't look that hard. Didn't 'spect to find nobody."

Dodge knelt closer. "If I'da knowed she was here, I'da been lookin' all day. Want me to take her off yer hands, boss?"

Ben stood, shooting Dodge a dirty look and wishing for the hundredth time he could just shoot him. "We've got her. Go back to sleep, Dodge." Ignoring Dodge's curse, he turned to Wade. "I'll see if Cookie's got any more leftover biscuits. Let her sleep. If she's been hiding scared, she hasn't slept much either. Take my bedroll. I'll be back after watch."

* * * *

Victoria turned over, grimacing at the stone that dug into her hip. She missed her bed. Hearing low murmurs and the sounds and smells of breakfast cooking, she knew Frank would be waking her soon. Too tired to face another day of riding, she burrowed into her bedroll. It seemed to take forever to get to Montana.

If Frank and James got them lost one more time…

A sob escaped as the horror came rushing back. Frank, James, Will, and Buck were gone. Dead. And the coyotes. "No!"

"Ma'am? Ma'am, wake up."

She came fully awake at the sound of an unfamiliar voice, sitting up with a jolt to find one of the big men from yesterday kneeling next to her. Did she know his name? She didn't remember. Scrambling out of the bedroll, she eyed him warily. "What happened?" The events of the previous night rushed back to her in pieces she struggled to assemble.

Tearing her gaze from his, she looked around the camp. There must have been at least two dozen men sitting around eating breakfast and drinking coffee. They didn't speak much, only low murmurs to each other but several smiled at her. Many stared at her curiously. She couldn't believe she'd slept so peacefully with all of these strange men so close by.

Even though the man who came to his feet next to her was the one who helped her last night, she still didn't trust him. His strength showed in every line of his body and in the careful way he moved. He could break her in half with no trouble at all.

From his wide forehead to his strong jaw, his features, too masculine to be considered handsome, drew her in a way she didn't understand. She couldn't afford that. Watching him warily, she searched the area around her bedroll. "Where are my boots?"

He smiled, a flash of white in a darkly tanned face. "Easy there. My name's Wade Beaumont. Nobody's gonna hurt you, I promise." He lifted the corner of her bedroll to expose her boots, turning each one upside down and shaking them before handing them to her. "I stuck 'em in here so no little critters would get inside. Just sit tight, and I'll get you some grub."

"Where are my knives?"

Wade pointed to where her knives sat on top of a rock a few feet away. "Thought you'd sleep better not wearin' 'em. You're not gonna pull one on me again, are you?"

Still wary, she forced a smile. "Not unless I have to." She sat back down on the bedroll and pulled on her boots, scrambling back to her feet to retrieve her knives.

The other large man approached and she remembered he'd also helped her. "Did you tell me your name last night?"

He handed her a plate of food and sat down on a log a few feet away with another. "My name's Ben Beaumont. What's yours?"

The smell of the food made her mouth water, and she wasted no time digging in. Forgetting her manners, she answered as she ate. "I'm Victoria Fowler, but everyone calls me Tory." Still not entirely trusting him, she didn't sit on the log next to him. Instead she sat on her bedroll.

The man who'd introduced himself as Wade came back, handed her a cup of coffee and went to sit on the log with Ben. "Victoria. Tory. That's a beautiful name."

Shoveling food in as quickly as possible, Tory kept her eyes on the men, aware of the stares of the others. "Beaumont? Are you brothers?"

Ben nodded. "Don't bolt your food. You'll get sick. There's plenty more."

Wade's look of concern did strange things to her stomach. "Yes, ma'am. I'm real sorry about your brothers. Can you tell us what happened?"

Tory struggled to swallow past the lump in her throat and had to take a sip of coffee before speaking. "We stopped here to camp." She could still see James and Will sitting on the log Ben and Wade sat on now, arguing about who was the better rider. Hurriedly wiping away tears, she forced herself to take another bite.

All of the men stopped eating to stare at her, only to glance away, looking uncomfortable.

"I'm sorry." She hated showing weakness in front of them. Sitting up straighter she put a hand over her knife, comforted by the feel of it.

Ben put his plate down and joined her on the bedroll, putting a hand over hers. "You have nothin' to be sorry about. Your kin got killed. Tell me somethin'. How did the coyotes get all of 'em like that?"

Tory shook her head, pulling away. "They were already dead when the coyotes came. Murdered by these men who showed up out of nowhere. Three of them. I think Frank shot one of them, but they all got away. I was at the pond, filling a pot when Frank yelled for me to hide. If I came out sooner to help them…When the men left, I checked them, and they were dead. I couldn't wake them up. Then the coyotes came, and I hid again. The sounds…Thank you for burying them. I didn't get finished before you showed up." She choked on a sob, wishing she had done things differently.

Ben lifted her chin. "Listen to me. If you came out sooner, those men would have killed you or did somethin' that would have made you wish you were dead. You survived, and that's all that matters. Don't think about the rest. Do you have any other kin?"

Pulling out of his grasp, Tory avoided his eyes. Not used to men like him, it disconcerted her that she felt so drawn to him. It would be wonderful to have his strength to lean on, but that same strength could easily be used against her. Butterflies took flight in her stomach as soon as he sat close and when he'd touched her chin, she'd felt it everywhere. She didn't know what it meant and didn't trust it. Or him. Or anybody.

She shook her head as the enormity of the situation hit her. "I don't have anybody else. We lived in Charleston. Daddy died of consumption and momma's heart gave out during the aggression.

When my brothers came home from fighting, they didn't want to stay there anymore. We sold everything and came out here to homestead. Those men took it all, the money, everything, even my clothes." She gestured toward her pants and big shirt. "Frank made me wear this and keep the hat over my hair so that nobody would know I'm a woman. He said it would be safer."

Ben stood and picked up his plate. "He was right. But he's gone, and you have no place to go, no kin to look after you. You'll have to come with us."

Tory came to her feet, uncomfortable with the way he towered over her. She took a step back and picked up her plate, quickly taking another bite. Who knew when she'd get the chance to eat again? Shaking her head, she shoveled food in as fast as she could, knowing they would be leaving soon. Not caring about manners, she spoke and chewed at the same time. "I've got to get home."

Wade moved to stand next to his brother, effectively blocking her view of the others. "What are you goin' to go back to? From what I've heard, it'll take a long time to rebuild Charleston. What would you do there?"

Tory stopped eating, staring back and forth at them. "What would I do if I went with you?"

Both men spoke simultaneously. "Marry me."

Silence fell over the camp, followed by low murmurs. Tory didn't know who looked more surprised. Ben and Wade stared at each for several long moments before turning back to her.

Ben smiled faintly. "Just come back home with us. We're only three days away. Once we get back home, we'll sort it all out. But I'm not leavin' you out here. You can go peaceful like or I'll tie you up and throw you in the wagon. Either way, you're goin'."

"Well that's real neighborly." At his lifted brow, she immediately regretted her sarcasm. In her present circumstances, she saw no other alternative, at least for now. It would give her a couple of days to think and she would at least have a place to stay until she made a decision. She hardly knew them, but for now they seemed safe enough to travel with. It had to be safer to travel with them than to remain out here alone. It didn't look like they'd give her a choice anyway.

She couldn't imagine marrying either one of them, though. She'd never met anyone so *hard* before. They obviously had to be to live out here and lived a life she knew nothing about. Their arrogance showed in their posture, their voices, even the way they moved.

Ben and Wade both looked completely comfortable with their authority and with their surroundings, as if confident they could handle anything that came along. She'd bet that if the men who killed her brothers attacked them, there would be a far different outcome. "If you don't mind, I'd like to go with you until I can figure this all out. I can't promise anything, though. I mean, I don't even know you."

Wade's smile made her heart flutter and caused a curious throbbing between her legs. "You won't be sorry. You can ride in the chuck wagon."

Nodding, she touched his arm. "Thank you. I'll try not to get in your way and help out as much as I can."

Ben clenched his jaw. "Ask Cookie for something for your face and stay out of the sun." Tossing the dregs of his coffee into a bush, he shot a look at his brother and strode away. His tone had a sharp bite when he yelled out at the others. "We're burnin' daylight."

Trembling, Tory stared after him. "Oh, no. I've caused trouble already."

Wade looked a little unsettled himself. "Don't worry about it. Everything'll work out just fine."

Tory watched him walk away and looked around at the others. They'd stared at her before, but now none of them would meet her eyes.

She knew next to nothing about any of them and she'd just placed her future in their hands. God help her.

Chapter Two

Wade looked out over the land he loved with pride and couldn't help but wonder what Tory would think of her new home. Every blade of grass, every tree and bush belonged to them. They'd paid for it with blood, sweat, and sheer determination.

He faced the same dirty, backbreaking work he did every other day on the trail, but knowing they'd finally crossed onto Beaumont land made the work a little easier.

After chasing down another cow that slipped from the herd, Wade rode back to his brother. "It's good to be home again, ain't it?"

Ben nodded. "It's still another day to the ranch, but at least we're finally back on our land."

Chasing down cattle that broke away as they crossed a stream kept them both busy for quite a while. It took another hour or so before Wade got a chance to talk to his brother again. Although he had a lot of work to do physically, it didn't take much thought and his mind wandered. Ben normally didn't talk much, but after this morning he appeared even quieter than usual.

Wade knew why. He'd seen the way Ben avoided Tory but snuck glances at her whenever he thought no one would see.

They'd be stopping soon. He wanted to talk to Ben before they did. A good sized pond lay about a mile or so away. Riding up to Ben and Red, he called out. "My mouth's already watering for the fish Cookie's gonna fry up tonight."

Red chuckled. "Yeah, but we're gonna hafta catch 'em. If Shorty tries, he talks so much they'll all leave." He took off to flush yet another cow out of the bushes.

Wade laughed, looking back toward the wagon and made a quick decision. "I'll bet Tory loves it here. I wonder if she likes fish."

Ben followed his gaze before turning back. "She'll eat it or Cookie'll make her do without."

"Neither one of us'll let that happen and you know it." When Ben didn't answer, Wade sighed. "The thought of what she went through still gives me the shakes."

"She did just fine. You'll take care of her now."

Wade inwardly cursed his brother's hard-headedness. "Damn it, Ben. I don't want a woman to come between us. If you want to marry her, do it. It's not like either of us has really gotten to know her yet anyway."

Ben barely glanced at him. "I see how smitten you are by her."

"Yeah and you're not? Even all sunburned and dirty, she's beautiful. And she's got sand. Most women woulda been hysterical, but she wasn't. Yeah, she was plenty scared, but I can't blame her for that. Watchin' her brothers die and then havin' to see what the coyotes done to them. Hell, a lot of men woulda been shook up."

Wade shook his head at Ben's continued silence. "Don't pretend you don't like her, too."

"Just leave it be, Wade."

Wade watched Ben take off but didn't miss the fact that his brother glanced over his shoulder toward where the chuck wagon brought up the rear. Ben spent so much time glancing over his shoulder today it was a wonder he hadn't been thrown. He knew his brother well. Ben wanted Tory for himself but would step aside so Wade could have her.

How in blazes could he be happy with a woman if he felt guilty about taking her from his brother?

Something had to be figured out and fast, before they *both* got too attached to her. What would they do if *that* happened?

Shaking his head, he rode in silence, fearing that it was already too late.

* * * *

Kneeling at the edge of the pond, Tory finished washing up the dishes, stacking them to take back to camp. She looked longingly at the cool water, wishing she could take a bath. Knowing the men waited for her to come back so they could do just that, she turned to go, almost running into Wade. "Oh! I didn't know you were here."

He smiled, reaching out to take the dishes from her. "I just wanted to make sure that nothin' happened to you."

Tory's face burned at his attention, and she hoped that her sunburn kept her embarrassment from showing. Used to being around more refined men, she didn't know how to handle this kind of attention, especially from men like them.

They sure didn't talk like any men she knew. She couldn't imagine any pretty speeches or flowery words passing their lips. They said what they meant and meant what they said. They weren't always polite, but they didn't talk in riddles either.

She still didn't know them well and struggled to adapt to their ways. From her conversation with Cookie, she learned they lived by a different code, one she didn't understand. "I'm fine. I'll just get going so you and the other men can use the pond." She started past him, but he stopped her with a hand on her bare arm. Little tingles ran up to her shoulder and beyond and, to her horror, made her nipples harden.

Wade stared down, moving his fingers back and forth over her skin. "You sure are soft."

Tory watched, mesmerized as his long fingers traveled over her arm and down to her hand. She knew she should pull away. He took too many liberties, but she couldn't find her voice to object.

He ran his hands over her fingers, frowning and lifted her hand to examine the rough spots. "Would you like to take a bath?"

Tory pulled her hand away, hiding her dry and calloused hands behind her back. She involuntarily glanced back at the pond, wishing she could sink into the cool water. Just the thought of taking off all of her clothing around so many strange men gave her the shivers. "No. I'll get a bucket of water when y'all are done and wash off in the wagon."

"I'll tell the men to wait a bit so you can have a bath."

Tory shook her head. "No. Y'all have been working hard, and I've just been riding in the wagon. You deserve it more." She turned and started back through the brush to the camp, more than aware of Wade following close behind.

"Cookie said you helped a lot with supper."

Tory didn't bother looking over her shoulder. Her insides fluttered, and she wanted Wade to kiss her so badly she shook. What would it be like to feel his firm lips on hers? She'd kissed a few beaus, but considered them boys compared to Wade and his brother. She yearned to feel Wade's strong arms around her and be held against his broad chest. Once in the clearing, her gaze flew automatically to Ben where he sat drinking coffee.

Heat coiled in her belly every time she looked at him. She'd never met a more dangerous man. But something in his eyes, in the way he looked at her, drew her like a moth to a flame.

She wanted so badly to be able to walk up to him and lay her head on his chest the way she'd seen her mother do with her father a hundred times. She didn't know what he'd do if she did that but didn't think she could handle it.

Ben stood and walked away without even meeting her eyes.

Why did that hurt so much?

As soon as they saw her, several of the men whooped and took off toward the pond, their arms loaded with a change of clothes and soap. She knew the others watched the herd and would run to the pond as soon as the other men relieved them.

Staring after Ben, she wondered what she'd done to upset him. She didn't think he liked her much and probably regretted bringing her with them. He'd seemed so sincere at the time, but now she wondered if he just considered her to be a burden. She didn't want to be a burden to anybody.

They gave her food, but she tried to make up for that by helping Cookie the best she knew how. She stirred what he told her to and collected firewood and washed up afterward.

Since Ben and Wade both appeared to be unmarried, they could probably use some help cleaning and cooking in their home. She would help out as much as she could until she could decide what she would do with her life.

Ben didn't speak as he went with the others, following at a much slower pace, not even glancing back. Wade placed the dishes on the back of the wagon and went to gather his things. "We won't be too long." He handed her a gun. "I'm leavin' this with you in case there's trouble."

Tory almost dropped it, finding it much heavier than she thought it would be. "I can't shoot anyone."

Wade's eyes narrowed. "You could if you had to." He ran a hand through his hair and sighed. "Just fire it in the air then. We'll hear it."

Tory nodded, looking around. "You don't think there's anybody around, do you?"

He smiled reassuringly. "No. And if there were, the men on watch will see them before they get here. Just keep it with you to be safe." He looked over to glare at John Dodge, who took his time gathering his things. "There are all kinds of animals around."

He waited until John went through the brush and followed him. Once he disappeared, she turned to Cookie.

"Aren't you going to go with them?"

Cookie gave her one of his rare smiles, showing several missing teeth. "Yes, ma'am. You did good today. You got grit for a girl."

Inordinately pleased by the compliment, she smiled, but quickly sobered. "You wouldn't have thought so if you could have seen me when those men shot my brothers. I was scared to death, so frozen I couldn't do anything. I couldn't even bury them before the coyotes..."

Cookie shook his head, rubbing his scruffy beard. "You woulda got kilt yourself. You did just right, hidin', and don't you let nobody tell you no different."

Tory nodded, blinking back tears. "Thanks, Cookie. You're a sweetheart."

"Aww, don't be talkin' like that. The men'll be thinkin' I'm soft."

Tory watched him go and poured herself another cup of coffee for something to do. She'd been using an extra bedroll and would have gotten it out if she hadn't been afraid of Cookie's wrath. They'd all been packed in the chuck wagon so tightly she knew she'd only make a mess of it if she tried to sort through them. He might be a softie about some things, but not the wagon.

She could hear the men laughing and splashing on the other side of the brush. It made her aware of her own stench. Except for Wade wiping her face two nights ago, she hadn't even rinsed off since a few days before her brothers were murdered. Now that the men would all be clean, it would make her own scent more noticeable.

The sponge bath she intended to take afterward would just have to do.

Several long minutes later, Wade appeared, wearing a fresh set of clothes and carrying his dirty ones, which he stuffed in his saddlebag. His long brown hair, now damp, had been slicked back to end between his shoulder blades, emphasizing his chiseled features in the faint light. "The others will be along soon, so you can have a bath."

"No, don't make them get out because of me."

Wade took the gun from her, sliding it into the front of his pants. "We'll be home tomorrow and they can get all the baths they want. Shorty says he has an extra pair of pants and Ben has an extra shirt. I washed out my socks and I'm gonna put 'em by the fire to dry so you can wear 'em."

Tory couldn't wait to jump in the pond and feel clean again, but the thought of being in there alone in the dark made her pause.

"Maybe it's better to just wash off. I don't want to be alone and ..."
She lowered her face, embarrassed at the thought of being naked
while surrounded by all the men.

Wade grinned, his gaze raking over her. "Don't you worry none
about being alone. Either Ben or I will be with you, and we'll keep
our backs turned. Nobody'll see you."

If either one of them wanted to force their attention on her, they
could have done so at any time. None of them could be called
gentlemen, but she had to admit they'd been very gentle with her so
far. She would have to trust them at some point. Right now her future
lay in their hands. Besides, she really wanted to feel clean again.

The men started coming back in a steady stream, Ben along with
them. His expression looked harder than ever, his glance cool as it
touched on her. His hair had also been pushed back, darker than
Wade's but not quite as long. Ben's brown eyes, darker than Wade's,
appeared almost black.

Turning away, she accepted the items Wade handed her, relieved
that it included a cloth for drying. She hated getting dressed while still
wet. "Thank you." Glancing around, she smiled at the now jovial
mood. "The men all must feel better after their dip."

To her annoyance, John Dodge approached. "I'd be willing to
stand guard while Miz Fowler takes a soak."

Just the thought of it made her shudder. Tory took an involuntary
step backward, not liking the look in his eyes. She did her best to stay
as far from him as possible. He'd been sneaking back to ride along the
chuck wagon several times today, always bragging on himself and
making lewd comments. Even his smile looked mean, and she didn't
trust him one bit.

Ben and Wade both stiffened. Wade touched her arm and turned
her toward the pond. "Much obliged, John, but you just go on with
Ned and help gather some more firewood."

John's eyes narrowed. "I see how it is. The boss man already
branded her for hisself."

A silence fell over the camp as both Ben and Wade stopped and turned to glare at John. Ben took a step forward. "Don't bite off more'n you can chew, Dodge."

Red, one of the older hands, came forward and shared a look with both Wade and Ben. "Come on, Dodge. Leave the woman be."

A chill ran up her spine at the evil look on John's face as the older cowhand led him away. Looking back and forth between Ben and Wade, she shuffled her feet. "I've caused you a lot of trouble already. I'm sorry for it."

Ben shot her a glance and turned away. "Go take your bath."

Wade lit a lantern before gripping her arm to lead her away. "Let's get goin'. When the others come off watch, they're gonna want a dip, too."

The heat of Ben's gaze burned her back until they got through the brush to the pond. As soon as she found herself alone with Wade, she started trembling. She'd never been in a situation quite like this before.

Wade smiled tenderly. "I'll turn my back. Let me know when you're in."

Tory nodded, too tongue-tied to speak. Keeping a close eye on Wade's broad back, she dropped her borrowed clothing onto a rock and started to undress, sticking her knives into one of her boots. She could hear the faint sounds of the men in the camp talking and Ned's harmonica as she finished undressing and moved toward the water, gasping as it touched her heated skin.

"Are you all right?"

Flicking a glance over her shoulder, she could see Wade still had his back turned. "Yes, I'm sorry. It's colder than I thought. I'm in now." Sitting on a flat rock several feet out covered her up to her shoulders.

Wade turned and sat on another rock, staring straight out to her left and showing her his profile. "Did you say your brothers fought in the war?"

"Yes. Will lost an arm and came home about the time my father fell ill. Frank, James, and Buck didn't come home until after he'd already passed."

"Where were you gonna homestead?"

Tory dunked her head before answering. Using the small bit of soap, she began to wash her hair, relaxing more by the minute. "Frank said somewhere in east Montana. He kept the map with him. I looked for it afterward, but the men must have taken it."

She rinsed her hair and hurriedly began washing the rest of her body with the little scrap of soap. As much as she'd like to stay in the water, she knew the other men would be coming soon and didn't want to remain unclothed any longer than necessary.

Standing up in the shallow water, she watched to make sure Wade didn't look as she vigorously washed herself, biting her lip to smother a gasp as her hands moved over her breasts. Her nipples hardened from the cold and felt much more sensitive than normal. The place between her legs tingled unbearably. Standing with her legs slightly apart, she washed herself there, shocked at the feel of her soapy hand on the slickness she found.

She finished washing, her face burning at the sensations like none she'd ever experienced before. Her skin felt too tight for her body, too hot. Her thoughts drifted to what it would feel like to have Wade's touch on her bare skin instead of her own.

She lowered herself into the water, rinsing the soap from her skin, hoping the cool water would relieve her. "I'm done. I'm going to get out now."

Wade stiffened and nodded. "That's fine. Be careful on the stones. Some of 'em are sharp."

Tory slowly made her way out of the water in the semi-darkness and started for her borrowed clothes, relieved when Wade made no attempt to turn around. Keeping her eye on him, she quickly dried off and picked up the shirt.

When something touched her hand, she looked down. Horrified to find a huge snake staring back at her, her mind went numb for several long seconds. When the huge snake moved, it shocked her out of her stupor.

Instinct took over and she screamed, running toward the only safety.

* * * *

Wade sat on the rock, shifting uncomfortably as Tory bathed in the pond. His cock pushed at the rough material of his pants, as hard as the rock he sat on. He'd give anything to be able to shuck his clothes and join her. He could well imagine sliding himself into her and feeling her tight wet sheath tremble all around him.

It had been too long since he'd visited the whorehouse in Texas and his body demanded release. It probably wouldn't have mattered if he'd fucked today. The most beautiful woman he'd ever seen stood only feet away, naked and wet, and his cock knew it.

He knew damned well Ben felt the same way and the thought of it cut him like a knife. Ben stared at Tory as though he could eat her up alive.

She would be a fine addition to their ranch and the new life they'd made. He wished she had a twin so they could each have one of her.

Trying to think about something else, he asked about her family but couldn't concentrate on anything except the sounds of her splashing and moving through the water. Hell.

The announcement that she would be getting out made his cock jump to attention. Hearing her move through the water, he smothered a groan. Just a slight turn of his head and he would be able to see Tory completely naked and wet. He'd bet anything that the light from the lamp made her wet curves glow. Keeping his head from turning had to be the hardest thing he'd ever done in his life. Not trusting himself, he squeezed his eyes closed, trying hard not to imagine moving to her and folding her into his arms.

Her scream of terror sliced through him, startling him so badly he almost fell off the rock.

His eyes flew open, he stood, and started toward her with his gun in his hand, all in one motion. He didn't even have time to blink as he caught her in mid-air as she threw herself at him, his arms going around her automatically. Struggling to hold on to the wet, wriggling armful of female literally climbing up his body, he searched the darkness for whatever frightened her.

Tory clamped her arms around his neck, nearly strangling him. Her legs went around his waist as she buried her face in his neck. "S-snake. In my clothes. A big snake."

"What happened?"

Wade turned his head at his brother's harsh tone, one hand on Tory's bottom to hold her, his gun pointed toward the rock where her clothes lay. "She says there's a snake in her clothes." Seeing several of the men running through the brush, Wade ordered them back.

Ben already had his gun drawn and came closer, looking toward the pile of clothes, but his gaze kept moving back to Tory. He glanced toward the brush, his features turning to stone. "Get back, Dodge. We'll take care of it."

"Yeah, boss. I'll bet you will."

Ben moved toward the rock as the large snake slunk away. He picked up the clothes, shaking them out before bringing them over.

Wade stood there, not quite sure what to do. He'd never been so close to heaven. Breathing in her clean, fresh scent he involuntarily tightened his hold on her bottom. The soft firm globes never stilled as she writhed against him.

"It's on my back. Get it off. Get it off." Her voice held a trace of panic that shook him.

Wade could see that the sight of her affected Ben more than he'd ever imagined it would. Ben stared at her hungrily, apparently unable to look away.

Tearing his eyes away from his brother's tortured face, he looked

down her back. "There's nothing on you, Tory. It's just your hair."
His words fell on deaf ears as she continued to squeal hysterically.

She continued to whimper, twisting frantically as though to throw
it off.

Holding onto a wet, wiggling woman proved no easy feat. With
his gun in one hand and trying to hold onto her with the other, he
didn't have a free hand to push the hair off her back. "Damn it, Ben.
Give me some help."

Ben looked up as though being snapped out of a daze and
swallowed heavily. Reaching out, he ran his hand over Tory's naked
back, gripping her hair and lifting it off of her. "It's just your hair,
Tory. Look. Look at me. Look, Tory. It's just your hair."

Ben's low, calm tone finally got through to her. She slumped like
a puppet whose strings someone cut and turned her head to look at
him. "It's just my hair?"

Wade hid a smile at the way Ben's gaze kept sliding up and down
Tory's naked back. His own hand tightened repeatedly on her slick
bottom as his cock nearly burst the buttons on his pants. He'd never in
his life been as physically excited. Blazes, he could spend the rest of
his life just like this.

Ben released her hair, smoothing it over her shoulder, his hand
lingering before he realized what he was doing and jerked it away.
"It's just a bull snake. They're not poisonous. You probably put your
clothes on top of him. Believe me, he's more scared of you than you
are of him."

Tory dropped her head on Wade's shoulder with a groan. "I can't
believe that. I—Oh! I'm—Holy juniper."

Wade held onto her as she tried to scramble from his arms,
something inside refusing to let her go. "Don't worry none. You got
scared. There's nothin' to be embarrassed about. Calm down."

Ben stared at her as though mesmerized and, to Wade's surprise,
tentatively reached out a hand.

Wade felt the shudder that went through her at the touch of Ben's hand on her back. He lowered his gun hand, leaving her back bare for Ben's caress.

He didn't know why he did it but for some reason it felt right.

The look of awe on Ben's face as he moved his hand slowly up and down Tory's back had the strangest effect on him. Something inside him warmed at the pleasure Ben apparently got from seeing and touching Tory. It excited the hell out of him to hold onto her naked little body while Ben touched her, speaking softly to calm her. The thought of sharing this kind of intimacy with his brother, the thought that they could both pleasure her this way made his cock even harder.

They'd shared women in the whorehouse when there hadn't been enough women to go around, but the thought of sharing a woman he cared about with his brother, who obviously cared for her, too, turned him inside out.

The fact that Tory buried her face in his neck, holding onto him tightly and no longer attempted to free herself from his arms gave him hope. In a move he knew could bring all of this to an end, he slowly turned his hand until his fingers grazed her slit. He desperately needed to know if she trembled from fear or pleasure.

His fingers slid through her juices, immediately becoming soaked.

Her soft moan as she trembled even harder made his cock jump. Relying on instinct and hoping he wasn't about to make the biggest mistake of his life, he thrust her toward Ben. "Here, hold her a minute."

As he'd hoped, Ben automatically caught her against him, looking like a man who'd found paradise.

Wade tucked his gun back into the front of his pants and took the clothes Ben had dropped when he'd caught her. "She's soaking wet."

"Of course she's wet. She just got out of the pond. Give me something to dry her off with."

Wade shook his head, smiling at the way Tory held on to Ben. "Not that kind of wet. Feel for yourself."

A look of disbelief crossed Ben's face as Tory moaned softly and hid her face in his neck. "Tory, is that true? Do you like when both Wade and I touch you?"

Tory's reply was muffled against Ben's neck. "Put me down."

Wade caressed her back now, bending to put his lips to her shoulder, meeting Ben's eyes. "Are you a virgin, Tory?"

"Y-yes. I'm not a loose woman."

Ben cupped her bottom, holding her against him as he stroked her back. "She's tremblin'. Tory, there's nothin' to be afraid of."

Wade shook his head. "Tory's not afraid of us, are you, darlin'? You like the way we're both touchin' you, don't you. You like Ben's fingers strokin' you." He bent to kiss her shoulder again, careful to keep his voice low. "Just keep quiet so the others don't hear you and we'll make you feel good."

Tory looked over her shoulder at him, the combination of trepidation and need in her eyes almost more than he could stand. "What are you going to do?"

Ben closed his eyes, gathering her close, the look on his face one that Wade had never seen before. "Will you let me stroke you there? I promise not to hurt you or to take your virginity. I just wanna touch you. Will you let me?"

Tory leaned back to look up at Ben, and although Wade couldn't see her face, the way she caressed her brother's cheek told him all he needed to know. With a moan, she buried her face against Ben's neck again and tightened her hold on him.

Wade met Ben's shocked gaze. He reached around her with one hand to steady her and moved his fingers lightly over the curve of her breast with the other. His cock throbbed at the sounds she made as he caressed her. "You have the softest skin. I could touch you all day."

Ben slid his fingers through her folds, drawing a moan from her. "That's it, sweetheart. Shh."

Wade's hand got caught between Tory and Ben's chest when Ben pulled her close to kiss her. He didn't know why the sight of Tory in his brother's arm this way excited him so much. They'd shared women in the past, but neither cared anything about them. This quickly became much more than he could have ever imagined. Unable to stand it anymore, he released his cock from its confinement and took himself in hand.

Lightly rubbing her nipple drew sounds from her that excited the hell out of him. He stroked himself faster, groaning as he came hard. He'd never needed it more.

Opening his eyes again, he took in the sight of Ben holding Tory close with one hand and stroking the place between her legs with the other.

Wade fixed his clothing and wrapped an arm around Tory's waist to take her weight and pull her slightly back against him, leaving room between her and his brother. It gave him room to explore her full breasts while giving Ben a chance to get a better look at her.

Ben broke off the kiss and adjusted her for better access, earning a cry from her that made Wade's cock stir again.

Wade smiled when she dropped her head back on to his shoulder. "Shh, darlin'. We don't want the others to hear. Gimme that mouth." He wanted to explore every part of her and at the same time swallow the cries she would make when she came.

She turned her face toward him and opened to him immediately, allowing him entrance and all but melting against him. Her cries and moans became louder and more desperate, telling him just how much she liked what Ben did to her. Her pebbled nipples invited his touch and she arched, wrapping an arm around his neck and pressing her breasts more firmly into their hands.

He'd never known a more responsive woman. It drove his own hunger for her even higher. Combined with the satisfaction at finding a woman that he and his brother cared for, his need became something he hardly recognized.

She tasted so good, soft and sweet, like no woman he'd ever kissed before. She didn't know how to kiss and the tentative stroke of her tongue on his nearly took off the top of his head.

Suddenly she stiffened and he swallowed her cries of pleasure as they forced her over the edge, her soft whimpers and the shivers that racked her body making him feel ten feet tall.

He lifted his head to look down at her, cursing the fact that it grew too dark to see her clearly, but what he could see filled him with a satisfaction he'd never known.

"I can't believe I let you do that to me." Her soft, breathless voice affected him like a stroke to his cock.

Wade turned her in his arms and held her closely, running a hand up and down her back until she stopped trembling. "Ain't nothin' wrong with lettin' us touch you this way. Now if anyone else tries to touch you like this, we'll have to kill him." At her startled look, he touched his lips to hers and set her carefully on her feet.

Ben handed her the pile of clothing. "We'd better get on back before someone comes lookin' for us."

Wade hid a grin as Ben touched his lips to Tory's hair before moving away, his mind going in circles. He wanted Tory badly and as much as he would deny it, Ben wanted her, too.

She'd fallen apart in their arms, not hiding anything from them and with no pretense. Even naked and frightened, she'd trusted both him and Ben to keep her safe and allowed them to touch her like no man ever had before.

A surge of possessiveness washed over him, the same possessiveness that glittered clearly in Ben's eyes as he watched her dress.

Wade would do anything to keep her. The thought of sharing her with Ben, the two of them taking care of her and building a life with her, filled him with a sense of rightness that was as fulfilling as it was unexpected.

His mind whirled as he started to plan.

* * * *

Tory's hands shook so hard it took her longer to get dressed than it should have. Her face burned at what she'd allowed them to do to her, but even now she wished she could still be in their arms. Her insides felt too hot, her breasts felt too swollen. Even the slide of the material over her nipples burned, making her stomach clench even tighter and gave her a fluttery feeling inside.

She couldn't believe her body was capable of what they'd made her feel. It amazed her, the pleasure so great she hadn't cared about anything else. Her legs still felt wobbly as she stepped into the borrowed pants, and she sat down so she wouldn't fall.

She wanted to curl up against one of them and feel their arms go around her, holding her until this strange vulnerability passed.

Once dressed, she turned and started back to the camp, aware that both men followed. Still shaky, she watched her steps, walking slowly so she didn't trip. As soon as they got through the roughest part of the brush, she involuntarily looked over toward John Dodge, breathing a sigh of relief that he sat with the others. Although he looked up immediately, he drank coffee and played cards with the others so he must have been there for some time.

She'd been afraid he'd been hiding in the brush and spying on them.

Ben held the lamp high so she could see better. "Stop starin' at Dodge. You're givin' him ideas."

Tory stopped in her tracks and whirled on him. Shaken by the way both of them had taken over her body just moments before, angry and confused because she'd allowed it, and disconcerted by the way she still trembled, she took it out on him. "I'm not encouraging Mr. Dodge. He gives me the willies. I don't trust him. That's why I watch what he does. You're his boss, aren't you? Can't you handle your own men?"

Ben handed the lantern to Wade and wrapped an arm around her waist to pull her against him, his voice deep against her ear. "I can handle my own men, but I don't want you stirrin' 'em up. Every one of 'em wants to get you naked.'

Tory could never remember being so hurt, so mad, made worse by the fact that she couldn't shake his grip. "I don't encourage them. I thought what happened back there meant something to you, but obviously not. If you or your men think I'm that kind of woman y'all can get that out of your heads right now!"

He raised a brow mockingly and licked his fingers.

She couldn't believe he'd be so crass as to remind her. His hum of appreciation at the taste made the place between her legs tingle with remembered pleasure. It had been a life changing experience for her, and it meant nothing to him. "Oh! Let go of me, you brute."

Tory almost fell when he released her. She shook off Wade's attempt to help her and glared at both of them. "Both of you better stay away from me. As soon as I can, I'm going back home."

Wade caught her before she could stomp away and leaned down to whisper in her ear. "You're not goin' anywhere, darlin'. You belong to us now. And you're gonna stay right where we put you. Encourage any of my men and you're signin' their death warrant."

Speechless, Tory kept her head down as they made their way back to camp. She wouldn't stay with bullies, and she didn't want anyone to get hurt because of her.

She wouldn't stay with men who thought so little of what she'd allowed that they would make fun of her for it.

As soon as they got to their ranch, she would leave the very first chance she got.

Chapter Three

Tory grimaced as John Dodge approached the wagon yet again. He'd been doing it ever since they'd started out that morning. She'd brushed him off each and every time, but he still kept coming back, his words cruder every time he opened his mouth. It made her wonder just how much Ben and Wade had told him about the incident at the pond.

With his gaze on her breasts, John rode closer. "We'll be home in a bit. I got me a nice little house all picked out. We can get the preacher to come out and settle in right quick."

Tory sighed, grateful that the kerchief she wore over her nose and mouth hid her distaste. Now she understood why the men wore them. The amount of dust the cattle kicked up amazed her. "No, thank you."

"So you just wanna spread your legs for the bosses, huh? That night you went to the pond they put the Beaumont brand on you, didn't they?"

Tory looked over at him. "I don't know what you're talking about. I took a bath and they scared away a snake that got into my clothes. Leave me be." The thought that he might know what they did to her made her feel sick.

He pulled his own kerchief down, flashing yellow teeth, the meanness in his eyes giving her chills. "Don't lie. You spread your legs for both of 'em. Know what that makes you? But it don't make no never mind. As long as you only spread 'em for me from now on, I'm willin' to overlook it."

Cookie said something under his breath she couldn't make out and then raised his voice to be heard over all the noise. "That's real nice of ya, Dodge, but I think you ought to get back to work. The bosses ain't gonna be happy with you lazin' off and botherin' the woman."

John Dodge's face hardened, making him look even meaner and more ruthless. "Stay out of it, Cookie. This is between me and her. Unless you've been pokin' between them thighs, too?"

Furious, Tory wished she had good aim with the knife so she could throw one at him. Still upset that she'd forgotten the one she'd hidden at the pond, she didn't want to take a chance on losing another. She held on as she went to the back of the wagon to find something to throw at him.

* * * *

Ben looked back at the wagon as he'd done dozens of times since they'd started out this morning. Furious, he jerked the reins. Damn it. For about the hundredth time he regretted hiring John Dodge for this drive. The man was just more trouble than he was worth. He'd put up with him because he'd needed the hands, but once they got home, he would send him packing. Glancing around, he saw Wade in the distance, also looking back toward the wagon.

With a wave, he gestured his brother to go deal with it, but Wade shook his head and rode off to deal with another breakaway.

Damn it. Why the hell didn't his brother go take care of his woman?

Enraged, he urged his horse faster toward the wagon. He didn't want to spend any more time than necessary with Tory, especially after that episode at the pond. He'd never get the feel of holding her, naked and wet in his arms, out of his mind.

Hell. He hadn't been able to go ten minutes without thinking about it. The memory of her, soft and wiggling against his chest and the way her juices had soaked his fingers as she found her pleasure came to him even in his dreams.

Her threat to leave infuriated him. She wasn't going anywhere and the first chance he got, he would prove it to her.

Damn and Blazes. He had no rights at all with her. She belonged to Wade. Approaching the wagon, he lowered his kerchief.

Cookie noticed him first and gave a satisfied nod.

Dodge was too busy ducking the pieces of firewood Tory threw at him while trying to keep his horse steady to notice Ben approaching. "Stop it! Don't try to act all prim and proper with me. I know you're the kind of woman who likes havin' a man between her legs. I bet you're one of 'em that squeals and hollers when a man's pumpin' inside you, ain'tcha?"

"Dodge!"

Ben didn't even try to mask his fury, letting Dodge see the full extent of it. "Apologize to the lady right now."

Dodge clenched his jaw and glared at her before turning to him, a fake smile plastered on his face. "Aw, boss. I didn't mean nothin'. I asked her to get hitched. A man's got the right to ask, don't he?"

Ben moved his horse between Dodge and the wagon, forcing the idiot to the outside. "Not this one."

"Is that right? I guess she must spread her legs real good for you and your brother to be fightin' over her."

Ben's hands tightened into fists on the reins and before he knew it, he'd shot out a fist, pulling his punch at the last second. He didn't want to knock Dodge out and have him ride in the wagon the rest of the way. "Ride on ahead to the ranch and tell Jeb we're comin' in."

Dodge nursed his jaw, glaring at him. "Keep her then. She's too damned much trouble anyhow."

Ain't that the truth?

He waited until Dodge cursed and rode away before turning to look up at Tory. Damned if she didn't look pretty as a picture even dirty and madder than a wet hen. Holding a piece of firewood in one hand, she held on with the other as the wagon bumped along. Disheveled, with her braid half undone and her eyes spitting fire, she made him hard as a rock. Shifting in the saddle, he moved closer.

"Are you all right?"

Tory nodded and sat down. "I can take care of myself. You and your men are a bunch of animals, and I can't wait to get back home where the men know how to treat a lady."

Ben clenched his jaw, the pain of her words like a knife through his ribs. It added an edge to his voice he didn't try to disguise. He looked pointedly at the firewood still clenched in her hand. "Ladies don't go 'round throwin' firewood. You're not goin' anywhere. You're gonna stay where I put you until Wade can deal with you. Men out here ain't nothin' like the dandies back East. Something you'll find out if you keep pushin'. Cookie, as soon as you get to the ranch, give her to Mary." He rode away without giving either one of them a chance to answer, too afraid she would see just how much he'd already begun to care for her.

Cookie's wife would take care of her. She and Cookie did all the cooking on the ranch and Mary took care of the house. She would get Tory something clean to wear and would keep an eye on her to make sure she didn't try to leave.

Just the thought of her trying to leave on her own scared the hell out of him.

She would be lost without someone to take care of her. Green as grass, she knew nothing about the wilderness or how to survive. Look what happened to her four brothers. If it hadn't been for a bit of blind luck, she'd either be dead or captured.

Damn fool woman. Like a stone in his boot, she made him uncomfortably aware of her every damned second of the day.

Still fuming, he rode purposely toward his brother, blaming him for not dealing with his future bride himself and placing him in the position of having to face her sharp tongue. "What the hell are you doing? Why didn't you go back to the wagon when I told you to? Didn't you see Dodge back there?"

Wade shrugged. "Yeah, and I knew you'd take care of it. What did Dodge say to her?"

"He told her he'd bet she was the kind of woman who screamed her pleasure when she had a man between her legs."

"Hell. Is she all right?"

Ben nodded, uncomfortable that the thought of Tory screaming her pleasure as he took her emblazoned itself on his mind. "Yeah. Looked mad as a hornet and threw firewood at him. It's a good thing we won't need it. I sent him off to tell Jeb we're comin' in before her aim got any better."

"We gotta get rid of him."

Ben glanced back at the wagon, cursing the fact that he couldn't go more than a few minutes without doing so. "Yeah, as soon as we get back."

They rode in silence for several minutes until Wade took off to get another cow that slipped away. When he came back, he moved close. "What do you think of Tory?"

Surprised, Ben glanced over. Wade knew him better than anyone and he didn't want him to see just how he felt about his brother's future wife. "She'll make you a fine wife, once you get her tamed." He tried to ignore the way his gut churned thinking about Wade claiming his marital rights with Tory. Taming the little hellcat would be a lot of fun.

Hell. Ben would have to move out of the house. He couldn't watch them go up to bed together. He couldn't lie there and not imagine her naked in bed with his brother. "I think I'll build myself a house. That way the two of you can have the big house when you get hitched. I'm gonna send for one of those mail order brides. I want to have the house done before she gets here."

Wade didn't say anything for so long, Ben wondered if he'd heard him. He wished one of the herd would break away so he would have a reason to avoid talking about it anymore. Of course now all the cattle behaved, and he didn't have to do anything more than ride beside them.

Wade turned toward him, his eyes crinkling. "You think Tory'll make a good wife, huh? So why don'tcha wanna marry her?"

Ben's jaw clenched. "What the hell are you goin' on about? You wanna marry her, don'tcha?"

Wade raised a brow. "Oh, she's mine."

Ben struggled not to show his jealousy. "Then there's nothin' to talk about, so quit yammerin'. Marry her and hobble your lip about it."

Wade shook his head. "I never said I was gonna marry her. I said she was gonna be mine."

Ben saw red. "What do you mean by that? You're gonna bed her and not take her to wife? Tory's no whore. She's still a virgin. You'd better not be thinkin' about takin' a virgin and livin' in sin." Ben hadn't punched his brother in years but wanted desperately to do it now.

Wade lowered his kerchief to take a drink of water. Wiping his mouth with the back of his hand, he looked over and grinned. "You're awful protective of her for someone with no interest in makin' her yours."

Ben didn't know why the hell his brother was going on this way, but it set his teeth on edge. "Are you gonna marry her or not?"

Wade's grin flashed before he pulled the kerchief back over his face. "One of us is." He took off after a runaway, leaving Ben cursing behind him. When they got back to the ranch, he would have to have a talk with Wade and figure out his brother's plans regarding Tory.

He saw her only briefly as they arrived at the ranch, sharing a look with Cookie, who raised a hand in understanding. Knowing that Cookie and Mary would keep an eye on her, he rode toward his foreman to give instructions.

As soon as he finished, he would take care of Dodge.

He glanced at his brother to see that Wade watched the wagon disappear through the gate, quickly turning away when he saw Ben watching him.

Why did Wade try so hard to hide his interest in Tory?

Shaking his head, he went through the gate. He would corner Wade tonight and get some answers.

* * * *

Feeling cleaner than she had in months and wearing a borrowed dress, Tory went into the kitchen to help Mary with the supper preparations.

Mary looked up from her biscuit dough. "Good. I knew that dress would fit you. It used to be my daughter's. Figured you were about the same size."

Tory grimaced. "I think your daughter's a little shorter than me. My father always said I'm too tall for a woman."

Mary looked surprised. "That's nonsense. Besides, the bosses are too big to have a tiny woman. If you was any tinier, they could carry you in their pocket."

Tory blinked, not knowing what to say. The bosses? "They just brought me here because I have nowhere else to go. I don't belong to either of them." It all hit her once again. "I really don't belong anywhere."

Mary wiped her hands on her apron and gestured for Tory to take over as she went to stir a pot on the stove. "Horsefeathers. Cookie tells me everything. You belong right here. Those two both took a likin' to you. Not too many women around here. If they're both taken with you, it's just smart to share you."

If Mary meant that she would play whore to both Ben and Wade, Tory knew she would have to leave in a hurry. "Share me?" She'd heard enough about the western territory to know that now that she lived on their land they could pretty much do what they wanted with her and nobody would be able to stop them. Fighting to hide her panic, she began to plan, angry at herself for trusting them

Mary looked up from her mixing. "Gettin' right common to share a woman in these parts. Only makes sense on account of there's not too many womenfolk around. Don't you worry none. The bosses'll take good care of you."

Tory couldn't believe it. After what happened at the pond, neither one of them showed her the tenderness they had before.

Wade kept his distance and Ben avoided her completely. Men didn't have to like a woman to be intimate with her. Her mother taught her that.

She'd definitely given them the wrong impression and could only blame herself. Weighing her options, she carefully kept her face down, not wanting to make Mary suspicious.

She'd have to take one of the horses. Mary told her how to get to town. If she left before it got dark, she should be safe and when darkness fell she could hide in the livery or behind one of the buildings. She'd really feel safer, though, if she could wear the clothes she'd worn before. "Mary, did you take my clothes?"

Mary nodded. "Yep. Put 'em with the clothes to be washed."

Tory tried to sound nonchalant, keeping her head down as she cut out the biscuits. "Where's that?"

Mary picked up a basket and started outside. "Don't you worry none about 'em. We'll deal with 'em on wash day. I'm goin' out to the garden. I'll be back in a bit."

Both Mary and Cookie watched her like hawks, and she knew Ben had been the one to order it. She would have to steal some food and something to carry water. Inwardly wincing at the thought of stealing even more from them, she rushed to the window to see Mary gathering vegetables. Grabbing a cloth, she quickly added an assortment of dried fruit, tied the ends of the cloth together and raced up to her room with it.

She ran back down with only seconds to spare as Mary came back in. Trying to breathe normally, she went back to the biscuits, careful to keep her face averted. She would try to stick a few biscuits in her pocket when she got the chance.

Struggling to appear calm, she wondered about her neighbors in

Charleston. If she could somehow make it back home, perhaps one of them would take her in. She could cook and sew to earn her keep.

She wondered how many of her neighbors still remained in Charleston. Scared at what she would be facing while traveling alone, Tory pushed it aside. She would take one step at a time and worry about problems as they came up.

She would have to escape at the first opportunity, before Ben or Wade took her virginity.

* * * *

Ben came down the stairs, anxious to see Tory. He'd rushed through the bath he'd desperately needed to get to her, surprised that Wade hadn't beat him downstairs. If she belonged to him, he would have been in a damned hurry to get to her.

Hell. He *had* been in a damned hurry to get to her.

He walked past the front room, looking in. When he didn't see her, he headed for the kitchen. "Mary, where's Tory?"

Mary looked up from the stove, her face wreathed in smiles. "She went upstairs to fetch you and Mr. Wade. It sure is nice havin' another woman around the place. Cookie explained everything. Makes perfect sense to me. Not too many women in these parts."

Ben normally could tolerate Mary's chattering but not this time. He involuntarily looked at the ceiling as if he could see through to Wade's bedroom. Having some idea of what the two of them would be doing up there, Ben felt like he'd taken a kick to the gut. He sat down, looking down into the coffee Mary handed him. "You're mistaken. Wade's gonna marry her."

Mary stopped fluttering around the room to stare at him. "But Cookie said—"

Ben stood, not wanting to hear any more. "Cookie got it wrong. I'll be out with Jeb. Call me when supper's ready." He started out only to stop short when Wade walked into the kitchen.

"Where's Tory?"

A chill went up Ben's spine. "I thought she was with you."

Wade's brows went up. "Why would you think that? I haven't seen her since we got here."

Ben whirled on Mary. "I thought you said she came up to get us for supper. I didn't see her and neither did Wade. Did you see her go up the stairs?"

Mary's eyes went wide. "No, but she finished with the biscuits and when I said I was gonna call you, she said she would go get you. I thought it was real romantic. When she went that way, I didn't pay her no never mind."

Ben and Wade both ran upstairs and checked everywhere for her. Ben ran back down to the kitchen, his brother close behind. Ignoring Wade's look of panic, he struggled to keep his voice low and calm, not wanting to upset Mary. "Don't worry. We'll find her."

He and Wade shot out the back door as if the hounds of hell chased them. They quickly spread the word that she was missing and within a matter of minutes every available man searched for her.

Ben shouted toward the stable. "Saddle our horses!"

It took several precious minutes before one of the men reported that his horse disappeared when he went into the bunkhouse to talk to Jeb. With all the footprints around, it took several more minutes before they could figure out the direction she'd taken.

Ben continued to survey the ground. "She's headed toward town."

When one of the hands brought their horses, he and Wade mounted and wasted no time giving chase.

Wade's voice shook. "I hope we find her before something happens to her."

Ben didn't even want to think about something happening to her before they could reach her. "Damned greenhorn. When we find her either you paddle her ass or I will!"

Chapter Four

Tory couldn't believe her luck. After finding a horse already saddled standing right outside the stable door, she took off in the direction of the nearest town and never looked back.

She didn't have a chance to steal any biscuits, but the dried apples and crackers in her pocket would be enough for now. Ben and Wade would be after her to get their horse back so she had to move fast. Horsefeathers. She wouldn't be able to stay in town after all.

She didn't have time to find her clothes either so she had to hike her skirt up to ride. A rifle in the scabbard gave her a small sense of security, but she hadn't looked in the saddlebags yet. If she got lucky she would find a change of clothes in there. Remembering what her brothers told her, she knew she'd get less attention if she dressed as a man. Nobody paid attention to a small, quiet man with his head down.

Scanning the distance, she made her plans. If she just dropped the horse at the livery and asked directions to the next town, Ben and Wade would think she'd left again and that would be the end of it. She could hide somewhere, rest and think about what to do from there.

That should work, especially if she could find some pants. After several minutes of riding, Tory's unease grew when the sun started to set. She'd been so intent on escaping she hadn't given any thought to the time. Heading west, she followed the gradually disappearing sun, fighting her panic. Once the sun set she would have no sense of direction. The thought of being out here in the middle of nowhere in the dark scared her spitless.

Fear of losing her virginity tonight made her take a chance she hoped she didn't regret.

She could almost hear Frank scolding her. Her brothers warned her repeatedly that her impulsive nature would get her into big trouble one day.

She didn't even know how far she would have to go to get to town. Did it lay west or northwest? Southwest? If she veered off the smallest amount or didn't veer when she should, she could miss it completely.

The stars! Frank taught her about finding the right direction by looking at the stars. She slowed her horse as the final rays of daylight disappeared on the horizon and searched the sky. If she could find the North Star, she should be able to find west.

Not a star in sight. Horsefeathers. What should she do now?

Hearing a howl in the distance, Tory tightened her grip on the reins, remembering the coyotes and the awful sounds they made.

She could do this. If she kept the horse going straight she should hear the noise and see lights from the town very soon.

Her heart sank when she remembered that the small towns she and her brothers went through in the last several months had been nothing like Charleston. Except for the saloon and the whorehouse, everything else would be shut up tight.

When the first drops of rain hit her, she wanted to cry.

She slowed the horse even more, not wanting him to trip on anything in the darkness, jumping at each little sound she heard. Thankfully it hadn't started raining hard but by the sound of thunder in the distance, she knew it might at any time.

She rode a little farther before it registered that the thunder never ended. In fact, it seemed to get closer and closer. That wasn't thunder. It sounded like horses!

With a cry, she urged the horse faster, bending over his neck as she tried to outrun them. Remembering what happened to her brothers, she choked back sobs as she searched frantically for signs of the town. If only she could get there before they caught her.

But they just kept getting closer. She turned to look just as her horse faltered and the next thing she knew, she flew through the air, landing hard on her back in the tall grass. Struggling to breathe, she heard shouts as the horses came to a stop close to her.

If she stayed quiet, maybe they wouldn't find her.

She remained motionless, trying to draw enough air.

"Tory! Where the hell is she? The horse threw her in this direction. Tory! You'd better answer me right now!"

Tory closed her eyes, resigned. Wade and Ben had caught her and Ben sounded furious.

"I've got her horse. He's not hurt."

Tory squeezed her eyes even tighter. Wade didn't sound any happier. If she could just stay still, maybe they would miss her. Only now they had her horse. She would be on foot.

In the dark.

In the rain.

Lost.

A whimper escaped before she could prevent it and she bit her lip to prevent another one. She could do this. She'd stayed quiet while those men shot her brothers and when the coyotes came. She would just stay right here and wait until morning to start walking to town. How far could it be?

The footsteps got closer and closer. Keeping her eyes closed, she hoped they would pass her by. When a hand touched her arm, she jumped, crying out, and tried to scramble to her feet. Another hand gripped her other arm, preventing it.

"Are you hurt?" Wade's voice held a hint of panic.

Tears of failure burned her eyes. "No. I don't think so. Just got the air knocked out of me. How did you find me?"

Both men continued to move their hands over her arms and legs, sending her senses on overload. Ben put a hand on her shoulder. "Tracked you. Then we just followed the sound of the horse. With all the noise you made, it wasn't that hard. I'm gonna pick you up. Let me know if anything hurts."

Still shaken, Tory tried to pull away. "I'm fine. I told you, I just got the wind knocked out of me."

Ben lifted her as though she weighed nothing and carried her to Wade who already sat on his horse. He lifted her to his brother with an ease that amazed her.

Wade settled her across his lap, covering her with a slicker like the one he wore. "Are you sure you're not hurt anywhere?"

The bite in his voice belied his tender words, telling her just how furious he'd become. Holding herself stiffly, she kept her voice low, not wanting to provoke his temper. "I'm just a little bruised from being thrown. I can ride my own horse."

Wade tightened his hold and started out. "No."

Tory leaned into his warmth as her teeth began to chatter. It rained lightly but steadily now and the wind blew a little harder. "Why not? I'm not hurt."

Wade urged the horse a little faster. "One, we don't trust you. You'll be guarded now to make sure you don't try to do this again. Two, we won't know how badly you're hurt until we get you back home and check you over. Three, it's not *your* horse. It's ours. Do you know what the penalty is for stealin' a horse?"

The moon peeked out from above the clouds allowing her to see the faint outline of his jaw. "I wasn't going to steal it. I was going to leave it at the livery for you."

Ben moved his horse closer. "What did you plan to do after that?"

Tory automatically opened her mouth to tell him and thought better of it. She might get another chance. "I'm not telling you my plans."

Wade's hand slid over her hip. "You'd better not have no more plans. You won't be able to get away from us again. Why'd you try to leave? I thought you was gonna stay with us."

Tory shifted but Wade only tightened his hold. "I found out what you two have planned for me. I won't make it easy for you, and I'll get away somehow. I won't be treated that way."

Ben's outline became more visible as the light rain slowed to a drizzle and the clouds parted even more, revealing a full moon. "What do we have planned for you that would make you run away?"

Thankful that because he leaned over her, his shadow hid her burning face, Tory told him. "Mary said that you wanted to share me. I'm a person, not something for you to play with."

Ben cursed.

Wade's body stiffened. Neither man spoke for such a long time that it made Tory nervous.

Wade's hand on her hip inside the slicker warmed her skin and sent her heart racing. The rain eventually stopped, and as the clouds parted even more, she could see their faces a little better.

Wade began to caress her hip and thigh, heating her skin wherever he touched. "What if Ben and I wanna share you? What if we want you to be our woman? Neither one of us would treat you like a toy. One of us would marry you, but you'd be a wife to both of us."

Tory blinked up at him, not sure she'd heard right. She'd never heard of such a thing before. "That's impossible. A woman can't have two husbands. Besides, what if you want to marry someone else?" She felt Wade shake his head.

"Ben and I have both taken a likin' to you. Women are scarce around here. The only ones we know of are married, too old or workin' girls. Think about it, Tory. You have no kin, no place to go. If you stay here, you'll have a nice place to live, two men to look out for you, and one of us'll marry you so you have the protection of our name."

She looked over at Ben who hadn't said a word. "Ben doesn't even like me. Why would he want to do this?"

Wade stopped the horse when Ben moved closer.

Ben reached out a hand and slid it under the slicker to touch her thigh. "I like you just fine. I stayed away from you so my brother could have you. But if you don't want this, I'll move out and leave you two alone."

Tory could hardly breathe. With both of them touching her this way, she thought she might just go up in flames. Tremors racked her body but not due to the cold.

Ben removed his hand, leaving her feeling bereft. "It don't matter who marries you. We'll both be gettin' a woman to warm our bed and give us little ones."

Tory hadn't thought that far ahead. "And you won't mind not knowing who the father is?" She couldn't believe he'd actually asked that. She wouldn't even consider something like this. Would she?

Wade's hand slid over her stomach. "They'd all have the same blood, the same last name. They'd all be ours."

Why did the thought of that make her heart flutter? Is this the way they lived out here?

If she did as they wanted, her life would either be heaven or hell. Tory shook her head. "You need to find another woman. I don't fit in here."

Wade slid his hand down to the hem of her skirt and lifted it to bunch at her waist. "You're the right woman. Ben and me both want you like crazy and you want both of us, too. If just one of us has you, the other won't be able to stand bein' around. It's either both of us or neither one of us. Where would you go if you didn't stay with us?" Both men brought their horses to a stop and stared down at her as Wade held her cradled against his chest.

Tory held her breath as Wade's hand slid upward and worked under her clothes. She gasped when he touched her bare slit. "What are you doing?"

Wade chuckled. "Showin' you just how much you're gonna like having both of us in your bed."

Tory couldn't believe the sounds that came from her own throat as Wade found her center and began to push his finger inside her. When she tried to close her legs, Ben held them open with a hand on each thigh.

Wade's finger pushed against the proof of her virginity, making it burn. When she hissed at the pain, he backed off, but kept his finger pressed against it. "Ben's gonna marry you, and I'm gonna take this. That way you'll know you belong to both of us."

Mortified, Tory hid her face against Wade's chest. "You shouldn't touch me that way. What are you doing to me? I can't do this with both of you." Heat flowed through her, making her forget she'd ever been cold. She shuddered when she looked down and saw that Ben watched what Wade did to her.

Wade laughed softly. "You don't understand yet, do you? I'm gonna slide my finger out so Ben can slide his inside you. I want him to feel your virginity, too."

Tory couldn't believe how her body reacted to his words. She wanted to be naked with both of them, to feel their hands on her like that night at the pond. A surge of need welled up inside her as her body craved the pleasure she knew they could give her.

Wade slid his finger out of her and reached for the buttons of her shirt, unbuttoning them deftly and spreading the ends wide. She heard a rip as the chemise tore and shivered as she felt the cool night air on her exposed breasts. "You belong to both of us. Just say yes."

Wade caressed one breast while Ben reached for the other.

Ben's rough fingers stroked a nipple, making her cry out. "I can't wait to see you naked in the light. Do you like havin' your nipples stroked?"

Tory threw back her head and arched, lifting her breasts for their touch. "Oh, yes. It feels so good." Something began to build inside her, just like before, something wonderful that scared her to death. "What's happening to me?" She shuddered as a hand slid between her thighs.

Ben kept stroking a nipple. "That's *my* hand between your thighs. That's *my* finger inside you. Do you want me to make you feel the way you did that night at the pond?"

Tory shivered as flames licked at her skin, touching her

everywhere. Knowing that both men would have the most intimate knowledge of her body and that both watched what the other did to her should have felt shameful and wrong. Instead it felt so good that all of her doubts faded away. "Yes. Please."

Wade bent to kiss the nipple he fondled, sucking it gently into his mouth and sending bursts of pleasure through her straight to the place where Ben's thick finger entered her body.

Her cries and whimpers filled the air as he pressed until it burned. "It hurts."

Ben's low voice sounded as though he was in extreme pain. "I'll make you feel better. All you have to do is say you'll marry me and let Wade and me share you. Be our wife, Tory."

Tory would have promised him anything as long as they eased her torment. She could escape when they least expected it. "Yes. Please. Something's happening to me. It's just like that night at the pond."

Wade lifted his head to stare down at her. The cool air on her moist nipples sent another surge of pleasure through her. "You'll belong to both of us forever, Tory."

"Yes, Yes. Please!"

Ben touched his thumb on a part of her made her jolt in Wade's arms. "We'll ride to town tomorrow and see the preacher."

Tory twisted in Wade's hold as Ben caressed something so sensitive she couldn't stand it. "It's too much. Oh!"

Her body gathered and tightened as a huge rush of the most incredible pleasure washed over her. Her cries and moans sounded loud in the night, but she didn't care. She just wanted it to go on forever. Her body jerked involuntarily as the pleasure crested. Tears pricked her eyes as Ben's strokes on her breast and her center gradually slowed until they stopped altogether.

Drawing enough air didn't seem possible. She lay limply against Wade as he buttoned her shirt.

Wade laid a hand over her belly. "That's twice we gave you pleasure, and we haven't even taken you. If I don't get inside you soon, I'm going to burst.

Tory didn't have enough breath to answer. Like a rag doll, she allowed herself to be passed to Ben for the ride home.

Ben pulled her firmly against him and tightened his hold as they started off. "When we get you home, we're going to make you feel even better."

Tory snuggled against his chest, unable to open her eyes. "Impossible."

Ignoring their soft laughter, she nodded off to sleep, breathing in his scent and secure in his hold.

* * * *

The sound of voices woke Tory. Opening her eyes, she struggled to sit up.

Red hurried forward. "Is she hurt?"

Ben handed her down to Wade. "We don't think so, but she was thrown."

Embarrassed, Tory struggled against Wade's hold. "I can walk."

Thankfully Wade lowered her to her feet. "Good. Now tell Henry you're sorry for stealin' his horse."

Tory looked up at him through her lashes. "I thought the horse belonged to *you*."

Wade lifted a brow at her sarcasm. "It does, but Henry rides her."

Resigned, Tory turned to the man Wade pointed to. "I'm sorry I took your horse, Henry. It won't happen again."

Ben gripped her elbow and steered her toward the house. "You can bet it won't happen again. Are you sore?" Before she could answer, he'd lifted her into his arms again to carry her inside. On the way through the kitchen, he called out to an anxious Mary. "The horse threw her. I don't think she's hurt, but we're gonna make sure. Fix me up a poultice and bring up some whiskey."

Wade followed closely as Ben carried her up to her room. Once inside he closed and locked the door as Ben lowered her to her feet.

When Ben reached for the buttons of her shirt, Tory tried to slap his hands away. "I can get undressed myself. I'm not hurt. You two shouldn't even be in here."

Ben leaned down until their noses nearly touched. "We've already seen you naked, touched you naked. We've touched your breasts and we've each had our fingers inside you. We've made you come. Tomorrow you're going to marry me and be a wife to both of us. We have the right to see you naked."

Tory lifted her chin defiantly. "Until we're married you have no rights with me at all. I want to be alone." She held her ground, hoping her nervousness didn't show as Ben's eyes glittered dangerously. She would never be able to adapt to the kind of life they wanted her to lead, especially dealing with men like them every day. They had more strength, both physically and in determination, than any men she'd ever known. They both made her so mad with their stubbornness she wanted to throw something at them.

She could just imagine what their reaction would be to that. Her brothers used to duck more items than she liked to think about.

Ben tapped her raised chin. "If you don't want us in your bed tonight, that's fine. It'll be the last time you refuse us. But I *will* see every inch of your body before I leave this room. I wanna see how bad you're hurt."

Wade moved to her other side. "You can let us help you out of those clothes or I'll rip them off. Either way we're not leavin' 'til we see you."

Tory knew they meant it. "Horsefeathers. You don't give me any choice about anything. Back in Charleston—"

Ben began unbuttoning her shirt. "We're not in Charleston. I'm not your brother or your daddy or any of the beaus you wrapped around your finger. You're a spoiled brat. Out here it's man's country and it's dangerous. You'll obey whatever Wade and I tell you to do or you'll go over my knee." He tossed her shirt aside as Wade took care of her skirt. "If you hadn't been thrown, that's where you would be right now."

Tory gasped. "You wouldn't! My daddy and my brothers never spanked me."

With his big hands on her shoulders, Wade forcefully pushed her down to sit on the edge of the bed and reached for her boots. "That's plain to see. Don't think you're gonna get away with doin' anythin' like you did tonight. You don't leave the ranch without permission and an escort. If you don't stay close to the house your rear end is gonna be so sore you won't be able to sit down."

Indignant over the way they so calmly threatened to spank her, Tory tried unsuccessfully to push Ben away as he and Wade finished undressing her. She may as well not have bothered. Before she knew it, they'd removed the last of her clothing. Wade stood at her feet while Ben toppled her to her back, holding both of her wrists in one of his and pulling her arms over her head, not allowing her to cover herself at all.

Ben never took his eyes from her body as he spoke to Wade. "Bring the light closer. I wanna see her better."

Tory couldn't just lie there while both men stared at her naked body. Tears of humiliation blurred her vision at the way her body tingled under their gazes. "Please stop looking at me. You're mean. Back in Charleston, no man would have the nerve to do what you two do to me."

Ben gripped her chin. "I keep tellin' you. We ain't in Charleston. You're our responsibility now. We'll do whatever we have to do to take care of you and keep you in line. Now be still so we can see if you're hurt."

Wade smiled gently. "You weren't scared earlier when we touched you. Why are you so scared now?"

Tory drew a shuddering breath. "I'm not scared. I'm mad and embarrassed."

Ben chuckled. "You're gonna have to get over it. We'll both be touchin' you all the time." He brushed his lips softly over hers. "Breathe, Tory."

Tory gulped in air, her tongue darting out of its own volition to touch his. His lips became firmer on hers, but still gentle as he explored her mouth with his own. He tasted so good, so masculine, and she kissed him back, allowing his tongue past her lips to touch hers. Hands covered her breasts lightly, moving gently to caress her and she squirmed, unable to lie still.

Ben lifted his head to look down at her. "I sometimes forget how tiny you are." He reached out to skim a finger over her nipple, startling a gasp from her.

"I'm not tiny. I'm too tall for a woman."

Ben laughed softly and lightly bit her lip. "You barely come up to my shoulder."

"That's because you're too big. Both of you." The sight of his big hand moving over her body did indeed make her look fragile.

Wade lay on the other side of her. "Just lie still so I can look at you. If I touch anything that hurts, tell me."

Hurts? She'd forgotten all about the fall. Her face burned at how quickly they made her forget everything else.

Ben lay propped on an elbow beside her. "There's no call to be shy. We've already seen you like this, remember?"

Tory hid her face against his chest. "I hate when you watch me."

Wade chuckled. "You keep your face hid then while I look you over."

Tory trembled as gentle hands moved over her, stroking and prodding.

Wade gently pressed against her ribs. "Does this hurt? Does it hurt here? No? Here?"

Tory kept her face hidden as Wade went over every inch of her skin. By the time he finished, she shook uncontrollably. She pushed her thighs tightly together to ease the ache that settled there and also to hide the fact that the place between her legs had become extremely damp. Again. How could they do this to her? And how could she just lie still?

"Turn over."

Tory whipped her head around to gape at Wade. "What?"

Wade's grin made the need worse. "I've only checked half of you. You fell on your back. I wanna see it."

Ben didn't wait for her to do it. He turned her over himself before she could move, once again amazing her with his strength. "Be still. This side's gonna be black and blue." He ran a hand over her left hip, his fingers stroking over her bottom. "Does it hurt?"

Tory grimaced. "Only when you press on it."

Wade checked the other side and got up to stand between her legs. Running his hands up each leg to her thighs, he squeezed gently, again asking where it hurt.

Tory buried her face in the quilt as she fought the riot of sensations that raced through her. Her body tingled everywhere, just like before. As Wade's hands slid up her thighs toward her center, she tried to push her thighs together again, but with him standing between them she couldn't.

Wade's hands covered her bottom cheeks, his thumbs sliding toward the dampness. "Tory's all wet again."

Ben pushed her hair back from where it hid her face. "Is that a fact?"

Tory turned her face away, unable to look at him. "Go away."

Ben bent to kiss her shoulder. "We'll let you hide tonight, but when we take you, you're gonna look at us."

Tory couldn't imagine doing such a thing. All of this felt far too intimate. Just when she thought she couldn't stand anymore, Wade knelt between her thighs and began kissing them. Startled, she tried to move away but their hold didn't allow it. "What are you doing?"

Ben lay beside her, pulling her against him and allowing her to bury her face in his neck. He kept one hand in her hair while the other stroked her back. "I think Wade wants to have a taste of you."

Tory froze. "What do you mean?" Oh God. What else could they do to her?

Ben kissed her hair. "He's gonna put his mouth where we touched you earlier and lick you."

Tory shook her head, but her body paid no attention. When Wade spread her legs even wider, her bottom lifted of its own accord. "He can't do that."

Wade lifted her, his hand gentle on her left hip, and placed a pillow under her belly. "Just trust us. I can see we're gonna have a lot of fun with you. You're always rarin' to go, ain't you, sweetheart?"

Fun? Rarin' to go? Tory didn't even get a chance to answer before he slid his tongue through her center. She cried out against Ben's neck, gripping him tightly.

Wade didn't even let her catch her breath before he did it again. And again. He licked her, even pushing his tongue inside her.

She couldn't even think. Her body shook and her brain went numb. Nothing mattered except where Wade's mouth touched her. When he began licking at that sensitive place that Ben stroked earlier, she screamed.

Ben held her face pressed against his neck. "Do you like that? Go ahead. Come, Tory."

She stiffened, her toes curling as that incredible feeling washed over her. Little pulses of lightning ran through her, making her body jolt and sizzle as she made the most unusual noises against Ben's neck. She couldn't seem to stop. Amazing pleasure went on and on, shutting out everything else.

By the time Wade loosened his grip and eased his strokes on her tender flesh, she could barely breathe. Weakly she pushed at Ben, trying to get air.

A knock at the door startled her. She'd forgotten all about Mary. Ben loosened his hold, running a hand over her back and kissing her shoulder. "Wade, get her into bed."

Weak as a newborn kitten and amazed at Ben's nonchalance, Tory allowed Wade to put her under the quilt. "I need to put on the gown Mary gave me."

Wade sat on the bed beside her, leaning over her. "No, you don't. You might as well get used to it because you won't be wearin' no clothes to bed from now on."

Tory's eyes flew open. "Sleep with no clothes on?"

Wade dropped a kiss on her mouth and grimaced as he adjusted his pants. "Tomorrow night Ben and I are going to touch every bit of you."

Tory's face burned. "You did that tonight."

Wade's smile made her heart skip a beat. "That we did. But tomorrow it's gonna be more. Ben'll wanna taste you like I just did before I take your virginity."

Tory couldn't even look at him. "I can't believe the way you talk. I can't believe you put your mouth down there."

Wade lowered the quilt to look at her breasts, dancing his fingers lightly over them. "This ain't the big city. Life's different out here. We're ranchers. We're blunt and know all about the act of breedin'. We don't know all the pretty words like back East, but we know how to take care of what's ours. You'll be provided for and have our protection. We don't like lyin' and we don't like games. There's nothing to be shy about in the bedroom. By the time Ben and I get around to doing all the things we want to do to you, you won't be blushin' anymore."

Tory raised her chin. "I don't know what kind of games you're talking about, but you and Ben do things to me that I've never even heard about. It scares me. My momma always wore her chemise to bed."

Ben came back with the poultice and a glass of whiskey. "Drink."

Tory pulled back and tried to turn her head away, but Ben cupped her jaw, forcing her mouth open and poured some of the whiskey into her. Tory slapped at him, coughing as fire hit her throat. "That's awful."

Ben held up the poultice. "Turn over."

Wade lifted the quilt and turned her over before she got the chance to do it herself. "You'll be plenty warm enough sleepin' between us. You won't need to wear nothin' to bed."

"Stop manhandling me!"

Ben leaned down until his lips touched her ear. "Baby, I ain't even begun to *manhandle* you yet." He applied the poultice and covered her up again. "Once you're no longer a shy virgin, we're going to handle you quite a bit. Get some shut-eye. Tomorrow we've got a lot to do."

Tory looked over her shoulder to watch them leave, feeling exposed with nothing between her skin and the clean-smelling sheets. How could they be so open about things like this? Having been raised to stay completely covered, she found it hard to adjust to having two men touch her so intimately without a second thought. They both did it so casually, and she could only imagine what it would be like once she became their wife.

Chapter Five

Riding back to the ranch, Tory kept glancing down at the thin band that Ben had placed there this morning. She found it hard to believe she was a married woman now.

Dressed in another borrowed skirt, she rode between Ben and Wade, her gaze flitting from one to the other.

Ben pulled her skirt down to cover her, making sure no leg showed before mounting his own horse. "You'll only be going to town and back. Just make sure you stay covered. You need new boots." Several of the hands joined them as the sun just started to lighten the sky.

While in town, the men came with them to see the preacher and had been witnesses. As soon as the ceremony ended, they left to run their own errands, leaving Tory alone with Ben and Wade. They hustled her around town, taking her to the general store to buy some material and thread for her. They introduced her to everyone as their wife. No one batted an eyelash, just wished them the best. Tory didn't think she'd ever get used to life out here.

Not used to asking anyone but her father or brothers for anything, Tory kept quiet as they gathered supplies. After the storekeeper measured her foot, Ben ordered new boots for her while she wandered around the store.

"Would you like to have those?"

Tory jumped guiltily at Wade's question. She'd been looking at a pair of denim pants like the ones back at the ranch. "Will I be allowed to wear mine?"

Wade smiled, his eyes twinkling. "You like wearin' 'em?"

Tory nodded. She hated asking someone else, especially someone practically a stranger for anything. "Very much. They're easier to move around in and I don't have to worry about my skirt flying up when I'm riding."

Wade nodded and helped her pick out two more that would fit her. "You can wear 'em inside the house or when you ride with us, but that's all. The rest of the time I wanna see you wearing a skirt. Do you need anything else?"

Tory shook her head, uncomfortably aware that they'd become responsible for her needs. They'd already purchased some linen for her to make a new chemise or two, along with other fabric.

Ben joined them and took her arm. "Let's go get somethin' to eat and start for home. Is there anything else you need?"

Again Tory shook her head, wishing for her own pocket money. In Charleston, her father always made sure she had enough money to buy a peppermint stick or a new hair ribbon. Now she would have to rely on her husbands for everything. *Husbands.* Even after what they'd done to her, she couldn't think of them as much more than strangers.

Strangers that she cared for and who'd somehow managed to take over her body, but strangers nonetheless.

If she helped out at the ranch, not only would they see her as someone they could talk to, but maybe she could earn herself a little pin money. If she could have a marriage like her mother's and father's, she would be content.

As soon as they'd eaten the chicken fried steak, potatoes, and biscuits, they got the horses and started for home. Within minutes, the hands from the ranch joined them.

The men continued to talk among themselves, mostly about people she didn't know. Ben and Wade added a comment or asked a question from time to time, but for the most part they remained silent.

As they approached the ranch, she got a really good look at the surrounding structures. She hadn't seen much when they'd arrived, instead watching the way the men herded the cattle. Last night she just took a horse and sped away, and it had been too dark to see much when they'd come back. This morning it had also been too dark and she really hadn't paid attention, too nervous about the wedding to really think about anything else.

The enormity of it hit her. She lived here now and this would probably be her home for the rest of her life.

Turning to Ben, she pointed to the sprinkling of structures in the distance. "What are those?"

Ben barely glanced at her. "Homes for some of the married hands. Stay away from 'em."

Hurt at his gruff tone, Tory knew she should have remained silent but couldn't. "I should go visit the wives. After all, I'm married to the bosses now." She slapped a hand over her mouth when she'd realized what she said. Did the other men know that she would be the wife to both of them? She knew marrying two men was against the law, but she hadn't really done that.

Ben seemed amused at her discomfort and leaned toward her, keeping his voice low. "They know, Tory." He straightened and this time didn't bother to lower his voice at all. "And they all know to stop you if you try to leave and to tell Wade and me if you do somethin' you're not supposed to."

Tory blinked. "How am I supposed to know what I'm not supposed to do?"

"We'll tell you. Just stay in the house and help Mary."

* * * *

Ben could feel his men's gazes and knew they thought it strange that he spoke to his new bride that way, but he didn't care. He didn't trust her not to try to run again and he didn't want her making friends with anyone who would help her.

He hated admitting to himself his lack of self-confidence with her.

He'd known plenty of women over the years and walked away after the sex without a problem. He hadn't even fucked Tory yet, and she had him spinning in circles. They'd rushed her into this without giving her a way out, making her think she had no other option.

Fear that she would try to run away again gnawed at him.

She didn't know that they would have helped her, even send her back East if she wanted, until that night by the pond. He hadn't been able to get the feel of her soft, wet body out of his mind. Those sounds she made not only made him hard as stone, but drew every possessive and protective instinct to the surface. Her softness, her scent and even her sweet voice with that irresistible accent made him ache to possess her. Wade knew it and led him straight to the preacher.

He couldn't believe his brother actually let him marry her.

Well, now that he had, they would keep a tight rein on her until she got used to the fact that she wasn't going anywhere. They would get her with child as soon as possible. Once a baby rested inside her, she'd never think of leaving again. Then, they could settle into a good life.

The way she went up in flames every time they touched her made him wild to have her. He and Wade learned a lot of things over the years and enjoyed sex in many ways with the whores in town. With a sense of pride, he knew that he and his brother had become downright popular at the brothel.

Because of their need for rough and raunchy sex, the painted ladies scrambled to be theirs for the evening. The thought of doing those things to Tory made his cock hard enough to pound nails.

Noticing the way the men kept sneaking glances at his new bride, he turned to glare at them, satisfied when they quickly looked away. Good. If they learned how possessive he would be of his wife, they'd stay far away from her. He didn't want any of them helping her get away either. "Pass the word. I'll use my bullwhip on anyone who helps her leave the ranch." Ignoring her gasp and the other men's incredulous looks, he rode in silence.

Once they got inside the gate, he got off his horse and dug through his saddlebags while Wade helped her down. He handed her the packages, his groin tightening as he looked down at her. Her sunburned face had turned a golden color and her lips now looked pink instead of red. Need made his voice rougher than he'd intended. "Put your stuff away in my bedroom. The top drawer's been emptied for you."

He walked away before he gave into temptation to haul her over his shoulder and carry her inside and straight to bed.

As Wade joined him at the fence, the men all moved away to tend to their chores, eyeing him warily over their shoulders. "Don't you think you're being a bit rough on her?"

Irritated with himself and with Wade for making him feel even worse, he looked around first to make sure no one would overhear him. "What if one of the women tries to help her leave? She could tell 'em about losin' her family and they would be all over themselves to help her get back home."

Wade grimaced. "Yeah, they would wanna help her, but when word gets around that she's ours, I don't think anyone would help her get away. I thought maybe you worried about what they would say about her havin' two men."

Ben shrugged. "I am, but it's gettin' more common around here with the shortage of women."

Wade smiled and slapped his shoulder. "Yeah, but they don't usually marry 'em. Congratulations. You're a married man."

Ben lifted a brow. "Even though your name's not on the paper, you're as much her husband as I am. I thought we'd agreed on that. So, congratulations to you, too." He sobered. "Wade, I want to know that if somethin' happened to me that you would go to the preacher right away and marry her."

Wade nodded. "Of course. She's mine now, too. I knew you wanted her. Would you really have given her up for me?"

Ben sighed. "I'd like to think so. I planned to, but to tell you the truth, I really don't know. Thank God we never have to find out."

Wade grinned. "I knew I could get you to see it my way." He grimaced and shifted his stance. "My cock's hard as a rock just thinkin' about taking her tonight."

Ben adjusted his own pants as his groin stirred. "I've been hard since that night at the pond. Let's get to work so we don't think about it."

Wade's eyes hardened. "I see how the men look at her. I like the bullwhip threat. It should scare 'em plenty. Everyone around here knows how deadly you are with that thing."

Ben shrugged. "Whatever it takes."

* * * *

Tory hardly touched her dinner, so nervous she knew she would choke if she tried to eat.

She'd helped Mary prepare it, thankful that the older woman didn't ask too many questions. Probably sensing her nervousness, she talked about mundane things around the ranch and asked what Tory thought of the town, thankfully not mentioning her thwarted escape.

Cookie came to collect his wife as he did every day after cooking supper at the bunkhouse, and the two of them left, leaving Tory alone with her thoughts.

She got shakier and more nervous with each passing moment.

Eyeing the wildflowers in the center of the table, she sighed. She'd married them and would learn to live with it. They both appeared to be more than capable of taking care of her. Hard men who would keep her safe and provide for her and her children.

Her pulse leapt and she closed her eyes at the thought of a child growing in her belly and how they would put it there. Her mother never told her about this wild hunger a woman would feel for her husband. She'd seen a lot of married couples that didn't even appear to like each other, but her parents hadn't been like that.

But they hadn't been like this either.

A loud noise at the kitchen door jerked her back to the present. Ben and Wade walked in carrying a bathtub. Wade shot her a smile. "Get some hot water on so we can all take a bath."

Tory rushed to do his bidding.

When they came back downstairs several minutes later, both went to the pump to wash their faces and hands, eyeing her with that look in their eyes again.

Sitting at the table with them, she picked at her food while both of them ate with enthusiasm. She resented their calm demeanors and remained silent as they spoke about ranch business.

Her skin felt too tight for her body. All she thought about all day had been the way they controlled her body as soon as they touched her. It felt so good, too good, but she hated the feeling of vulnerability. She'd been helpless to deny them anything and had to bite her lip to keep from asking for more.

Confused about her response to them and scared of what the future held, she'd been on edge all day.

Women weren't supposed to act that way and when Ben and Wade learned of her wanton thoughts, they would not be at all happy.

Their pride in her virginity, the way Ben covered her legs before they started out, and the way they glared at anyone who even looked at her told her they expected her to be the lady she'd been raised to be. But something happened whenever they got near, something that changed her.

They might forgive what happened at the pond because she'd been scared, but if her body kept betraying her the way it did last night, they would soon know for sure.

Finally her nerves stretched to the breaking point. "My father never spoke about work at the table."

Conversation broke off immediately as both men stared at her.

Mortified at her outburst, Tory stared down at her plate.

"Is that a fact? Look at me."

At Ben's cool command, Tory braced herself and looked up, not sure what to expect. To her surprise he nodded and reached for another biscuit. "I think it's a good rule. Consider it your first as lady of the house. You got any other rules we should consider?"

Inordinately pleased and relieved, Tory smiled and shook her head. "None that I can think of."

Wade covered her hand with his. "This is your home now, Tory. You're our wife. You're gonna hafta get used to that. You'll have a lot of responsibility here."

She stared down at his hand on hers, fighting the surge of pleasure it gave her. Both men had big hands, browned by the sun. Looking at their long, blunt tipped fingers, she shivered remembering just how those fingers felt pushing against her virginity.

She wondered just how much of them had actually entered her body. They would never try to put their entire finger inside her, would they? She could only imagine how much that would hurt.

With Wade's sleeves rolled up, his muscular forearms could be seen clearly. As brown as his hands, they looked strong, very different from her father's and her brothers'.

She witnessed their strength for herself but didn't think she'd seen the extent of it. She saw Wade carry a calf, for goodness sake.

Thinking about having two such strong, masculine men having free rein with her naked body frightened her more than she wanted to admit. They'd been gentle with her so far, but she'd seen the hungry looks on their faces and their insistence that she hide nothing from them. How would their strength be used on her when they were in the throes of passion?

Tory shook off her thoughts and blinked up at him. "What kind of responsibilities? I'll take care of the house, but I thought I would be expected to talk to the other wives. Since I'm not allowed to, I don't know what you want me to do."

Wade released her hand and shot a glance at Ben before going back to his food. "Just take care of the house for now. You'll meet the other women later."

"When?"

Wade clenched his jaw. "Soon. Just get used to takin' care of the house for now. Can you sew?"

"Of course."

"Good. We have a lot of things that need mendin', and Mary's hands give her too much trouble to do it. Eat your dinner."

Tory nodded and lowered her head again. She would carry out her duties as a good wife and wouldn't give them any cause to regret marrying her. She would gradually gain a little independence and make them see her as more than just someone to warm their bed.

Now that they'd stopped talking about the ranch, they finished the rest of the meal in silence, making Tory wish she hadn't said anything at all. Unable to stand it any longer, she rose from the table and started to clean up.

Ben gripped her arm and lowered her back to her chair. "Sit down. The clean up can wait 'til morning."

Once again amazed at his strength, she couldn't prevent him from lowering her to her seat. "I really should do it now."

Ben looked over at the stove and frowned. "Is that all the water you put on to heat? We need enough for all of us to take a bath."

He and Wade got up to put several more pots of water on to heat before sitting back down. "You can clean up until the water's hot. Then you're gonna go take a bath and get ready for bed."

Tory nodded, squeezing her thighs closed against the rush of moisture that gathered there. Just the thought of taking a bath while she was alone in the house with them sent her pulse racing.

Jumping back up out of her chair again, she started to clean up from dinner, uncomfortably aware of how closely the men watched her. Her gaze kept sliding toward them, even when she tried hard not to look at them. Her nipples hardened as they pushed against her chemise, and she fought not to rub them to relieve the ache. She could only imagine what they would think of her if they caught her doing that. She served them coffee and almost finished with the dishes when Ben got up to check the water.

His eyes moved over her breasts before they met hers again. "Go upstairs and get ready for your bath. We'll bring the water up and start some more."

Turning away, Tory nodded, wiping her hands and started for the stairs. She went straight into Ben's bedroom, where she'd put her things earlier. She got a towel and a bar of soap, wishing for one of the scented ones her mother always made for her.

An idea hit her. She hadn't seen any of the scented soaps in town. She could make them herself. It would be something else to do and she could keep some for herself and sell the others to the storekeeper. That way she would at least have a little money of her own.

Cheered by her idea, she opened the drawer that contained her things and pulled out a fresh chemise, looking up as Ben and Wade walked in, each with a big pot of hot water.

Ben poured his into the tub. "Don't get in there yet. It's too hot for you. I'll bring up some cool water next."

Wade eyed her chemise. "Put that away. You won't need it."

Tory's face burned. "But it's still light out."

Wade lifted a brow. "I already told you that you'll be sleepin' without any clothes on. We're your husbands now and have the right to see you naked whenever we want."

Ben smiled faintly, the look in his eyes making her tremble even more. "We're going to bathe you. By the time we're finished we'll have seen and touched all of you. No sense in being shy after that."

No one had bathed her since she was a little girl. She'd never heard of a husband bathing his wife. "You can't."

Wade turned from where he'd started to walk out the door and came back to her, lifting her hand and tapping her wedding ring. "You wear the Beaumont brand just as much as the cattle out there. You belong to us, and we can do what we want with you. Now get those clothes off. We'll be right back up."

Stunned, she stared after him, angry and hurt at the way he'd lumped her in with his cattle and more than a little frightened at the way her body responded to his cool tone. Her movements slow, she put the chemise back in the drawer and took her time arranging the things she'd gathered. Remembering what Ben had said about each of them taking a bath, she got two more towels and added them to her small pile.

We can do what we want with you.

She looked down at the ring on her finger, twisting it around. Wade spoke the truth. In the eyes of the law and of everyone who worked for them, she was now not much more than their property.

* * * *

Once back in the kitchen, Ben took a moment to lean against the table, adjusting his pants yet again.

Wade grimaced as he did the same. "I don't know how long I'm gonna be able to hold off. Maybe I should go take the edge off before I touch her again."

Ben straightened and looked out into the yard as the sun started to set. "She's more nervous than I thought she'd be. I know she's still a virgin, but with all we've done to her so far, I'd hoped she woulda calmed down some."

Wade joined him to look out the window. "Thank God she's one of those women who likes it. I shudder to think what woulda happened if she didn't. Damned if I want to spend the rest of my life tryin' to get inside a woman who's fightin' me off."

Ben nodded. "Yeah. She's wilder than most of the women in the whorehouse. I'm glad she's not like the other women I've heard about back East. Hell if I want ladylike in my bed. Every time I think about us takin' her together, I'm ready to burst."

Wade groaned. "Don't even talk about it. She ain't ready for that, and I don't even wanna think about it. I'm already on edge. I'd hoped Tory woulda been lookin' forward to tonight."

Ben nodded. "I did, too, but what the hell do we know about women like her? I was thinkin' if we bathed her first, we could loosen her up and get her used to our touch again. If we make her bathe us, she could get used to our bodies and won't be so scared."

Wade ran a hand through his hair. "It's a good idea. She ain't touched us yet, and I'm sure she has no idea what a cock even looks like. But I don't know if I'm gonna be able to hold off if she starts washin' me."

Ben didn't think he'd be able to hold off either. "I wonder if it'll scare her or help her if we come while she's bathin' us."

Wade groaned and bent over. "Fuck! Just thinkin' about it makes my cock ache."

Ben grinned and slapped him on the back. "At least it'll take the edge off. Come on, our bride's waitin'."

Ben walked back into the room to see Tory still fully dressed and testing the water. "I told you it was too hot. Why ain't you undressed?"

She hurriedly straightened and backed away. "I, um, I just got more towels." She pointed to a pile of towels beside the tub. Placing the scrap of soap and a small cloth for washing on top of them, she eyed both men warily.

Ben poured the cool water into the tub as Wade walked through the door with another big pot of hot water. "Put the towels on the bed so they don't get wet. Then get undressed before the water gets cold."

* * * *

Tory quickly moved the towels to the bed, eyeing the distance between the bed and the tub. Would she have to walk naked in front of them to get to her towel?

Ben finished pouring the water into the tub and set the empty pot by the door while Wade placed the other pot full of hot water next to the tub. Both men straightened and watched her expectantly.

Ben folded his arms across his chest. "Get those clothes off, Tory. We ain't gonna see nothin' we ain't already seen before."

Tory snapped at him. "That doesn't make it any easier." Immediately regretting her outburst, she lowered her eyes and began to undress. She took her clothing off slowly, grateful for the dimming light and the shadows that reached across the room.

While Ben stood watching her, Wade moved around the room and started lighting all of the lamps.

She stepped out of her skirt and laid it over a chair. "Why are you doing that? Isn't one enough?"

Wade turned from where he'd just lit another. "We want to be able to see you, and we want you to be able to see us. There'll be no hidin' in the bedroom, Tory."

Ben moved close to take the shirt she'd just removed and placed it on the chair with her skirt. "I want to see that beautiful face when you come, honey."

Tory shook even harder. "My mother told me that it would be painful and—" She snapped her mouth closed.

Ben smiled gently. "And what, honey?"

Tory shrugged. "And that a woman learned to lie still and accept it."

Ben moved closer, running his finger over her bare arm. "You're not gonna just lie there, darlin'. We already know that you're the kind of woman who likes it. Don't try and pretend otherwise. Now get the rest of those clothes off right now."

Mortified that they knew that, Tory lowered her gaze and finished removing the rest of her clothes, determined not to show her shameful need. Feeling too exposed, she covered her breasts with one arm and her mound with the other hand.

Ben bent sideways to test the water, his gaze burning her as she stood there completely naked. "Take your hair down."

To do that, she would have to lift both arms above her head. "I kept it pinned so it won't get wet."

"Take it down." The harsh demand in Ben's voice gave her no choice.

As she lifted her arms to her hair, his eyes raked over her naked form, making her even more self-conscious. With her arms up, her breasts lifted so that her nipples stood out.

Wade came up behind her, the rough denim of his pants brushing against her bare bottom. "No, don't lower your arms. Do what Ben said. Take your hair down."

Tory's hands shook as she began unpinning her hair, breathless at the way Wade's hands came around to caress her belly.

When they moved higher to caress the soft underside of her breasts, she couldn't bite back a moan and involuntarily started to lower her arms again.

Ben shook his head. "Keep your arms up until you find every pin."

Tory's face burned even hotter. It felt so incredibly naughty to stand there unclothed, facing Ben while Wade caressed her.

Ben took a step toward her as she desperately searched for the remaining pins. "Spread your legs." The underlying edge in his softly spoken demand excited her even more.

Tory pushed her thighs together even tighter as another rush of moisture escaped. Years of lectures on the proper behavior of a lady came rushing back to her as tears of mortification stung her eyes. "Please. I can't."

Ben's expression softened. "We don't wanna hurt you any more than necessary. We hafta learn what you like so you can like it, too."

Wade's hands moved higher to lightly stroke her nipples, making them burn. "We want you to come. Do you remember how good it felt when you did that before? Don'tcha wanna feel it again?"

Ben lifted her chin and bent to touch his lips to hers, demanding entrance. When her lips parted, he pushed inside, angling her head to his liking.

Tory's knees went weak, and she grabbed at his shoulders. When Wade lightly pinched her nipples, she cried out into Ben's mouth.

Ben lifted his head, caressing her jaw, while looking down at what Wade did to her. "You like that, don't you, honey? Keep your hands on my shoulders while I find the rest of the pins. I don't want any of the damned things in my bed."

Tory stood as still as she could while Wade fondled her breasts and Ben worked his fingers through her hair until he'd rid it of all the pins. Her hair tumbled down over her shoulder and to her waist, covering one breast.

Ben took the end of her hair and ran it back and forth over her nipple, smiling as she moaned. "Spread your legs for me, darlin'." When he slid a hand down and tapped her thigh, she knew she had no choice.

As soon as she opened her stance, placing her feet about a foot apart, Ben slipped a hand between her legs, his jaw clenching when he found her slick. "You *do* like this. Come on, let's get you into the tub so Wade and me can bathe you and see what else you like."

On shaky legs, and with their help, Tory got into the tub, anxious to sink under the water. She'd never been inside such a huge tub before. It amazed her that she could almost stretch her legs out all the way. As soon as she settled into it, both men took off their shirts and knelt on either side of the tub.

Wade caught her staring at their muscular chests. "There's no sense gettin' our shirts wet. Now lie back so I can wash your hair."

Trembling, Tory obeyed him, embarrassed that lying back pushed her breasts out. "Why are your chests so brown?"

Wade grinned and helped her sit up again. "We work with our shirts off a lot. Look how pale you are. You look so delicate. I'm afraid I'll break you."

Tory closed her eyes and moaned as he began soaping her hair and once again wished for one of her mother's scented ones. "I'm not fragile. I kept up with my brothers when they thought I couldn't do it."

Ben soaped the cloth and began to wash her neck and shoulders. "And you survived just fine until somebody could get to you. You're a brave little thing takin' on two husbands, too."

Tory gradually relaxed under their hands and smiled. "Cookie said I've got grit."

Wade finished and helped her dunk her head to rinse it.

With her eyes still closed, Tory wrung out her hair and sat back, placing it over the rim of the tub to dry.

Ben chuckled. "I wondered what you were gonna do with all that." He wiped her face with the cloth so that she could open her eyes. "Cookie's right." Soaping the cloth again, he began to wash the rest of her.

Every inch of Tory's skin tingled as he ran the cloth over her. It felt especially good as it rasped over her nipples.

Wade slid his hand under her, lifting her slightly so that Ben could reach more of her.

Ben ran the cloth lightly between her thighs. "I'm going to lick you right here. I'm gonna eat your pussy, darlin'."

Tory moaned and gripped the sides of the tub as Ben lifted first one leg and then the other, soaping every inch of her. She'd overheard her brothers using that word before, but no one had ever said it to her.

Finished, Ben quickly rinsed her. "Stand up."

With Wade holding on to her, Tory stood and started to step out.

Ben stopped her. "Not yet. I haven't finished."

Wade held her hair out of the way so Ben could wash her back. "No. Don't cover yourself. We've got every right to see you this way. There's nothin' to be ashamed of."

Tory's embarrassment lessened as Ben continued to move the cloth over her bottom and down her thighs, her body becoming looser with each pass of the cloth.

After Ben rinsed her and sluiced off some of the water, Wade lifted her out of the tub and began briskly drying her off. "Now you can wash my back." He tore the rest of his clothes off and stepped into the tub.

Tory's pulse leapt, her mouth going dry at seeing his cock for the first time. It looked much larger than she'd expected, so dark and menacing that it took every ounce of courage she could muster not to run from the room. Women did this every day. She could do it, too.

Lifting her eyes to his, she gulped, her heart racing at the determination in his steady gaze.

Then he smiled.

His smile warmed her, so gentle and affectionate it loosened some of the knots in her stomach. Drawing a deep breath, she smiled back tremulously. Just thinking about how many times she'd be asked to perform this chore made her insides flutter with anticipation.

A wife would be expected to wash a husband's back when asked, but she didn't know if she should want to do it just for the pleasure of touching him. Wrapping the towel around herself, Tory knelt beside the tub and picked up the cloth, accepting the soap that Wade handed to her. "Don't you want to change the water?"

He kept his expression neutral, but his eyes bored into hers with an expression she'd already learned to be wary of. It disappeared so quickly she'd wondered if she'd imagined it. He chuckled softly and sat up. "You weren't even dirty. Are you gonna wash my back or am I gonna hafta wait all day?" His grin took the bite out of his words.

She should have been relieved at his teasing, but it only made her want to touch him more. Careful to keep her upper arms down to hold her towel in place, she began to wash him briskly, trying not to let him see how badly she just wanted to stroke him.

Was it fitting for a woman to want like this?

When she finished, he scooted forward and bent back to wet his hair.

"Would you wash my hair for me?"

Shooting a glance at Ben, she reached for the soap again. "Of course." She found herself staring at Ben as she washed his brother's hair. She soaped it, running her fingers through the wet strands and rubbing Wade's scalp. Her nipples poked at the front of the scratchy towel, making her catch her breath. The sharp pleasure surprised her, and she tightened her thighs against the moisture that escaped from her slit.

"That feels real good, honey. I think this is gonna be your job from now on."

Wade dunked his head and sat back up, sending water splashing. Gripping her hand, he pulled her to his side. "I want you to wash my chest. I wanna feel your hands on me." He leaned back in the tub, watching her expectantly, his eyes hooded.

She jumped when Ben moved in behind her.

"Easy, honey. Wash Wade." His hands came around to cup her breasts, the action rubbing the rough towel over her nipples, sensitizing them so much she could hardly stand it.

Moisture coated her thighs as she soaped the cloth yet again. She couldn't take her eyes from Wade's body, roped with muscle. When he lifted his arms to rest them on the sides, she gasped at the sight of his cock pointing toward his stomach.

Her brothers talked to each other about that part of themselves enough over the years that she knew what to call it.

Wade took her hand in his and drew it to his cock, closing her fingers around it.

Tory's eyes flew to his as Ben gave the towel covering her a tug, making it fall to the floor. Her own desire melted some of her inhibitions, and she wanted desperately to please him. "W-what do I do?"

Wade covered her hand with his and began to stroke. "I want you to make me come before I take your virginity. I'm too hungry for you to be patient."

Ben slid one hand down to her center. "Nice and wet as always. You're a helluva woman, Tory. Take Wade's cock in your hands and make him come. Do you remember how it felt when you came? You'll make Wade feel that."

Excited, nervous, and intrigued, Tory reached out to tentatively stroke the tip of Wade's cock. When he gasped, she whipped her hand back, looking up at him in alarm. "I'm sorry."

Wade gripped her hand to bring it back. "It didn't hurt, darlin'. It felt too good. Do you remember what it felt like when I touched your little clit?"

Ben separated her folds, his thick fingers insistent as he stroked that part of her that made her gasp. "Stroke Wade the way he's showin' you, honey. Watch his face. Watch what you do to him."

Mesmerized, Tory couldn't look away. Thankfully, Ben stopped stroking what they called her clit so she could concentrate on pleasing Wade.

Ben propped his chin on her shoulder to watch what she did to Wade. He cupped her breasts, his hands warming them, making her shake as his thumbs moved closer and closer to her nipples. "No, honey. Don't stop. It feels real good to him. You're gonna make him come."

Tory couldn't have stopped if her life depended on it. "It's soft, like velvet but really hard at the same time." Biting her lip, her eyes flew to Wade's. She couldn't believe she'd said that.

Wade didn't seem to notice. He groaned, moving his hips in time to her strokes.

Ben's thumbs rasped over her nipples, sending a surge of pleasure to her slit. "It has to be hard to enter your body."

Tory gulped. It didn't seem possible. "I don't think it'll fit." Fascinated by the way Wade reacted to her touch and enthralled at the feel of the slick hardness in her hands, Tory redoubled her efforts.

Ben lightly pinched her nipples, rolling them between his thumbs and forefingers, shooting a stab of pure heat straight to her center. "It'll fit inside you just right. Women stretch. It'll only hurt a little the first time when he breaks your virginity. After that, it's all pleasure."

Wade's body tightened impossibly and he erupted, groaning loudly and startling Tory into releasing him. Ben grabbed her forearms, urging her back. "Don't stop. Nice, slow strokes."

Trembling, Tory did as he said, alarmed by the cream that shot out of Wade's cock and the look on his face as she slowly stroked him. After only a few seconds, Wade took her hands in his and washed them off, his eyes hooded. "Hell, darlin'." He blew out a breath and sat up, pulling her close for a kiss. "That's what'll happen when I'm inside you." He stood, lifting her into his arms and striding toward the bed, his eyes roaming over her. "Now I'm gonna watch Ben lick that pussy."

Tory shook with a mixture of fear and excitement as Wade laid her on the edge of the bed and ran a towel over his limbs before lying beside her. She knew just how quickly their touch would send her flying.

Ben quickly knelt between her thighs, lifting them over his shoulders and spreading her wide.

The first swipe of his tongue forced a cry from her, the unfamiliar and intimate touch on her sensitive flesh almost too much to bear. "So pink and soft. I've been thinking about this all day."

Tory tried to stay still as Ben used his mouth on her, but she couldn't. Grabbing on to the quilt, she dug her heels into his back. Struggling to be quiet, she bit her lip as he stabbed his tongue into her over and over.

Wade slid a hand over her stomach and up to her breast, bending to lick the other. "Don't hold back your cries. We wanna hear 'em."

Tory couldn't stand much more. Her body bowed as shivers of pleasure raced through her. Having experienced the ecstasy, her body craved it again, reaching desperately for that incredible sensation. The heat of Ben's velvety tongue caressing her so intimately made her burn. The tug at her nipples added more to the heat at her center, driving her closer and closer to the edge. Just when she thought she'd go over, Ben raised his head.

"No! No. No. No. Please." Tory couldn't stand it. Her body demanded the release that she knew he could give her. She needed it as much as she needed her next breath.

Ben stood and leaned over her, caressing her cheek as he brushed her lips with his. "It's better this way, darlin'. Next time I get my mouth on you, I'll make you come."

Wade pulled her to the center of the bed, took her hands in his, and raised them over her head, locking his fingers with hers as he moved over her. "Steady, darlin'. Nice and easy."

Tory squirmed restlessly but froze when he began to push into her, instinctively fighting it. The thought of him pushing all of that into her terrified her. The sensation of the blunt head pressing so intimately into her as both men leaned close, watching her face, overwhelmed her.

Ben leaned closer and stroked her cheek. "Don't tense up. Try to relax, honey."

Gulping in air, she met Wade's eyes as he pressed insistently into her. "It burns. Please stop. It hurts." She tried to fight him off as the pain overcame the pleasure.

Both of their faces looked harder than she'd even seen them, which scared her even more. Tears pricked her eyes at the unrelenting burn between her legs. Sobbing now, she tried to push him off.

Ben growled from beside her. "Do it."

With one powerful thrust, Wade ripped through her barrier, filling her completely.

Tory cried out, trying to buck him off. "No. It hurts."

Wade released her hands to gather her against him, raining kisses over her face. "That's the last time it'll ever hurt, honey. I swear it. Shh. It's over."

Ben stroked her arm, bringing her hand to his lips. "You're ours now."

Tory's body struggled to accept Wade's thick cock inside her. Realizing that he remained motionless and that the pain gradually lessened, she stopped fighting to lie limply beneath him. Those incredibly wonderful tingles disappeared, leaving her embarrassed and uncomfortable.

Wade held himself still, his expression harsh. "Does it still hurt?"

Tory's face burned. "No." She wished he would just get off of her.

Wade grinned and bent to kiss her. "Now the pleasure begins."

Tory tensed as he began moving, expecting the pain to resume. Instead, something inside her awakened, his cock moving over tender flesh, creating the most incredible sensation. Little by little her body loosened as each stroke felt better than the one before.

Ben leaned close, never taking his eyes from her face. "I'll bet you're so tight you're killin' Wade."

Tory didn't answer, turning her face away, embarrassed. Her imagination of such a thing had not prepared her for the reality or for the fact that they watched her intently the entire time. With all the lamps burning, they could see everything.

Wade cupped her cheek and turned her back to face him. "We wanna watch your face. Don't turn away again." His slow strokes continued, draining away the last of her resistance.

Wade's grip on her tightened. "So tight. Darlin' you feel so good."

Ben groaned, tightening his hold on her hand. "I can't wait to get inside her. Look at her."

Tory barely heard them, becoming so focused on the surge and withdrawal of his cock inside her pussy. Her body shook, her insides quivering with the need for more. Knowing Wade would give her what she needed, she tightened her legs around him and lifted into his thrusts, which came a little faster now.

The pleasure built and she arched, her body tightening as tingles of pleasure washed over her. The hoarse cry that ripped from her didn't even sound human. Her insides clenched on his thick cock, making her burn even hotter.

Her release hadn't been as strong as before but at least it no longer hurt. When the tingles started to fade away, Wade's hand under her bottom lifted her into his thrusts. "That's it, darlin'."

Tory panicked at how deep he went. After several strokes, it surprised her that the pleasure began to build again.

Ben rubbed her arm. "Let it happen, Tory. Let it take you."

Wade's thrusts came even faster, his face a mask of concentration as he took her there again. With a final thrust, he held himself deep, his low groan telling her that he'd found release inside her body.

After several long minutes, Wade lifted his head from where he'd buried it in her neck. "Are you all right?"

Tory tried to duck her head, but he wouldn't let her. She shrugged, trying to look everywhere but at them. "It only hurt at the beginning. I'm sorry I tried to push you away."

Wade's smile made her heart lurch. "You did exactly what I thought you would. That's why I held your hands. It's instinct. I'm sorry I hurt you, but I promise it'll never hurt again."

Tory nodded hesitantly, not knowing what to say.

Wade kissed her again, slow and leisurely. "Rest for a bit. Ben and I are going to dump the tub and put in more hot water." He lifted himself from her chest and slowly withdrew, grimacing at her wince.

Ben leaned over her, brushing his lips over her jaw. "I'm gonna get most of the dirt off so I can bathe with you. The hot water'll make you feel better. Stay put."

Tory didn't have any choice. Sore and tired, she closed her eyes, dozing as the men worked. One of them covered her with the quilt, but she didn't open her eyes to see which one. She drifted, comforted by the sounds they made as they went up and down the stairs and refilled the tub. She'd almost fallen asleep when strong arms slid beneath her and lifted her.

The quilt fell away as Ben carried her to the tub and sat, settling her on his lap, his hard cock pressing against her bottom. He leaned back, pulling her back against his chest and spreading her thighs as wide as the tub allowed. "Relax, darlin'. Let the warm water help."

Wade pulled up a chair and sat at the side of the tub to watch, and it relieved her to see he looked more relaxed, smiling when she tried to cover herself.

Leaning back against Ben with the evidence of his arousal pressing into her back, she couldn't stop squirming.

Ben chuckled and reached for the cloth, soaping it. "If you can't sit still, wash my back."

Tory accepted the cloth and stood to step out of the tub.

Ben gripped her hips to stop her. "No. Do it from right here." He sat up and gripped her thighs to urge her closer.

Bending over his shoulder to soap his wide back, she ran her slick hands over his sinewy muscles. With his lips moving over her thigh, it got more difficult to concentrate on her chore. Her movements slowed as he slid his hands up and down her legs.

"She's got the most amazing ass."

When Wade's hands slid over her bottom, the slide of the cloth over Ben's back slowed even more. She tried to straighten but stopped at Ben's rough growl. "Finish what you're doin'."

Both men continued to stroke her, seemingly fascinated by every inch of her flesh. It seemed to take forever to finish washing Ben's back, but she finally succeeded. He allowed her to straighten before tugging her hands. "Now my chest and I want you to work your way down to this." He stroked his thick cock that rose from between his legs. "Will you do for me what you did to Wade?"

Tory got her first good look at his cock. She couldn't take her eyes from the way he moved his hand over it. It looked every bit as large as Wade's, and she couldn't believe she'd actually taken something that size into her body.

"Tory?"

Tory blinked and met his eyes, nodding hesitantly when he lifted a brow. She hoped she'd be able to please him the way she had Wade. Right now, only pleasure connected them. She needed that connection. Kneeling between his legs, she began to soap the cloth again. When she began to soap his chest, he leaned back again, resting his arms on the side of the tub, watching her through hooded eyes.

Her nipples tingled under his gaze as she finished with his chest and shyly reached for his cock, which rose toward his stomach. Now that she knew what to expect, his groan didn't startle her as she took him in both hands and began to stroke him the way she'd stroked Wade.

Ben closed his eyes, moaning as he rocked his hips the same way Wade did. He didn't seem to mind that both she and Wade watched him in such an intimate moment.

She couldn't imagine ever being as comfortable with something so private.

It thrilled her that such a big, strong man like Ben could find such pleasure in her touch. The heady feeling of having him come into her hands excited her even more. She slowed her strokes the way he'd taught her and finally stopped. He lay there with his eyes closed, making her wonder if he'd fallen asleep.

When he finally opened them, the look of hunger in them stunned her. He leaned over her, carefully lifting each of her knees to place them over the rim of the tub.

Running his lips over her jaw, he made a place for himself between her thighs. "You're too good at that. Stay still. I wanna see if you're too sore to take me."

Tory held her breath as Ben lifted her bottom onto his thighs and ran a hand down to her center. She tightened on the thick finger that slid into her, automatically rocking her hips.

Wade knelt behind her, his big hands moving over her breasts. "Looks like she wants more."

Ben rubbed a hand over her stomach. "Do you want more, Tory?"

Tory couldn't fight the rising need and arched toward him, her body already craving the release she knew he'd give her. "Yes." Her eyes popped open as his finger slid out of her and he stood.

Lifting her, he ran the damp towel over her and strode back to the bed. He laid her on the cool sheets and moved between her thighs, nudging them apart. Reaching down, he watched her face as he traced her flesh softly as though afraid of hurting her.

The gentle way he touched her wiped away her trepidation. She closed her eyes and just let herself feel.

The bed dipped as Wade moved above her, lifting her hands over her head again. "I like seein' you all stretched out this way." Leaning over her, he took a nipple between his teeth, startling her.

"Don't hurt me."

Wade released her nipple to run the flat of his tongue over it. "Never. Didn't it feel good to have my teeth on you?"

"Yes. No. I don't know."

Ben ran his finger around her opening over and over before slowly pushing inside, at the same time stroking her clit.

She thrashed, tightening on his finger as he took her higher and higher. And then he stopped, withdrawing his finger and teasing her opening again. "Please. Oh, please!"

Ben stopped his torment and straightened, leaning over her and poising himself at her opening. "No. Don't tense up. It won't hurt this time. I promise." His words ended in a groan as he slid into her.

Tory's muscles loosened up when she realized it didn't hurt. When the strokes brought the pleasure back, she couldn't keep from moaning. Ben's strokes stopped as he studied her face. Tory bucked, trying to get him to move, ignoring Wade's soft chuckle.

Ben groaned again, his teeth clenched. "Does it hurt?"

Wade took a nipple between thumb and forefinger, pinching lightly. "Look at her. That ain't pain."

Tory tightened her legs around Ben as he started thrusting. His grip on her hips tightened as his strokes came faster and faster, rubbing along her sensitive inner flesh. She couldn't stop her body from clenching on his length, loving the way it filled her completely.

Wade ran his hand down her body and began stroking her clit as Ben dug at a similar spot inside her. Every inch of her body sizzled.

Everywhere they touched made her pussy burn even hotter. The pleasure got to be too much to bear and she flew, screaming Ben's name as she clamped down on him.

Her body stiffened and bowed, consumed by the raw bliss that spread through her. It shook her, this amazing need they created inside her. It got worse every time they touched her.

Ben's deep groan followed hers as he pushed deep, his cock pulsing inside her. His arms tightened around her as he buried his lips in her hair.

Too exhausted to open her eyes, she lay limply as they caressed her, praising her for how wonderful she'd been. She hadn't done anything, so she didn't know what they meant and didn't have the energy or the courage to ask.

Right now she cared about nothing but sleep.

Chapter Six

Tory crept down the stairs the next morning, embarrassed to have slept so late. She remembered Ben tucking the covers around her the night before and both of them slipping in on either side of her. After that, she remembered nothing.

She hadn't meant to start married life by sleeping half of the morning away and shirking her duties. Hurrying into the kitchen, she saw Mary working on lunch preparations. "Good morning. I'm sorry I slept so late. What can I do to help you?"

Mary smiled gently. "Don't go apologizin' to me. You're the bosses' wife."

Tory grimaced. "Were they real mad that I slept so late?"

Mary laughed. "Spent the whole time they was eatin' starin' at the ceiling like they was imagin' you still in bed. Both of 'em was grinnin' from ear to ear."

Not knowing what to say to that, Tory remained silent. *The way these people talked!* She would never be able to be as open with intimacy as they all seemed to be.

Tory spent the morning learning about her new home and helping Mary with the cooking. Before she knew it, Ben and Wade came through the back door for lunch.

Mary left them alone and went out to help Cookie serve the men.

Ben waited until they were alone before wrapping an arm around her and pulling her close. "How're you feelin'?

Tory's face burned at the intimate question. "I'm fine. I'm sorry I didn't get up to fix your breakfast."

Ben kissed her forehead. "You were plumb tuckered out. When

Wade and me got up, you never even moved."

"Sorry. It won't happen again. Lunch is ready."

Wade closed in on her other side, grinning mischievously. "Oh, it'll happen again, darlin'. There's nothin' to be sorry for. We wore you out. Are you sore?"

Tory ducked her head, not comfortable with this kind of conversation, especially in the light of day. "I'm fine." Thankful when they sat down, Tory served lunch and didn't breathe easily again until they'd finished and left.

Every time she looked at them it reminded her of what they'd done to her the night before. She kept dragging her eyes away from their hands and mouths, her face burning as she remembered how they felt on her body.

And now she *knew* exactly what lay behind that bulge in their pants.

Her mother would be horrified at the fact that she shared a bed with two men. That reminded her that she wanted to change the sheets. She'd seen the stain when she got out of bed this morning.

The afternoon passed in a flurry of activity that made her feel right at home. She didn't mind hard work but she needed to know what they expected of her. She'd had so many changes in her life in the last year, it felt good to go about doing normal chores again.

She just had to tip-toe around the rest until she figured it out. She had no experience with being married, especially to *two* men unlike she'd ever known. She also hadn't planned on the level of intimacy they demanded. She knew next to nothing about ranch life and didn't have any friends. It would take time, but an afternoon of normalcy and a chance to think made her confident she could do it.

Thinking about the money she hoped to make, she checked the soap supply to see that they had plenty. It would take a while to gather the flowers she needed and dry them for the soaps and sachets she wanted anyway.

She didn't even have an idea of what kind of wildflowers she would find around here or what they smelled like. It would be quite a challenge to sort them all out, one she looked forward to.

During dinner, both Ben and Wade patiently answered her questions about the ranch and some of the wildflowers. Everything had been going well until she asked again to meet some of the other women.

Ben's jaw clenched and his eyes went hard. "I said you can meet 'em later. Just stay in the house for the time bein'."

"But I'll be going out tomorrow with Mary so she can show me where to wash the clothes. She can't do it herself. You see how much trouble she has with her hands."

"Damn it."

Tory blinked at the bite in his tone. "I don't see why I can't talk to the other women. It makes me look like I think I'm too good for them. Y'all don't want that, do you?" A painful thought struck her. "You're ashamed of me!"

Both of them just stared at her in astonishment.

Wade recovered first. "Why would you think we're ashamed of you?"

Tory shrugged. "Well, you won't let me talk to anyone, not even the people in town. If everyone knows I've been intimate with both of you, are you afraid they'll think I'm a wh—"

"Don't say it!" Ben's tone chilled her. "It ain't nothin' like that. We don't trust you. You're gonna run off the first chance you get."

"I am not!"

Ben reached out and tugged her chair until she sat right next to him. Laying a hand over her stomach, he bent until their noses almost touched. "You might have a baby in here even now. Don't even think of leavin' with our child."

Tory gaped at him. "Is that all I am to you? One of your breeding stock?" She'd thought after the gentle way they'd taken her last night they would have begun to care for her at least a little.

Ben sat back and regarded her steadily. "What do you want to mean to us?"

So mad and hurt she couldn't think, Tory flew from the chair, knocking it over in the process. "I hate you. I hate both of you. And you're right. I'm leaving the very first chance I get."

Wade looked up from his plate. "You won't get the chance." He looked back down and took another bite.

His nonchalance infuriated her even more. Tory hadn't let loose with her temper in months, and it felt good to do so now. She picked up the water pitcher and threw it at Wade's head, ignoring his look of astonishment.

He ducked before it could hit him. It smashed against the wall, water spewing everywhere. When both men stood, she ran for the back door, aghast at what she'd done. She could almost hear her brothers chiding her again for being so impulsive.

Running outside, she headed for the stables, hoping she could hide in there until they cooled down. The look on their faces when they'd started after her scared her to death and made her regret losing her temper.

A glance over her shoulder showed them back far enough that she should be able to get inside before they caught her. They'd obviously stopped to put on their boots, something she wished she'd had the time to do.

The fact that neither one ran after her scared her more than if they had.

She ran into the stable and almost straight into Red.

"What are you doin' out here? Where're the bosses?"

Tory looked around for a place to hide. "Right behind me. Oh, Red, I lost my temper and threw a water pitcher at Wade. I just need to hide until they cool down. They're going to beat me for sure."

Red shook his head, running a hand through his hair, more gray than the red he'd been named for. His lips twitched as he looked toward the stable door. "The bosses don't hit women. But you prob'ly shouldn't athrowed a water pitcher at 'em."

Tory grabbed Red's arm. "Please, just tell me a good hiding spot until they calm down."

Red shook his head. "You're gonna hafta git outta this yourself. Got no call to come atween a man and his wife."

The door to the stable opened, slamming back against the wall. Ben and Wade strode in as calmly as if they'd just come out for a leisurely walk, but both of their gazes immediately went to her and sharpened.

Tory swallowed heavily and back away. "I didn't mean it."

Ben moved forward and leaned against one of the stalls with his arms crossed over his chest as Red headed for the door.

Wade took a step toward her. "You threw a pitcher at my head."

Tory took another step back and shrugged. "I missed."

Wade's brows went up. "Only because I ducked."

Tory took another step back. "I'm sorry."

Wade nodded. "You will be."

"Wh-what are you going to do to me?" She hated the tremor in her voice, but she honestly didn't know what to expect. With their size and strength they could hurt her so easily, especially being so angry.

"What do you think I should do to you?"

For every step he took, Tory took one back, but his long strides brought him closer each time. "I think you should accept my apology, especially if I promise to never do it again." That sounded reasonable to her.

Wade pursed his lips and appeared to give it some thought. "No. I don't think so. If I let you get away with it, who knows what you'll do next time."

In her panic, Tory decided to attack back. "It was your fault."

Wade stopped, his brows going up again. "How is it my fault?"

His calm demeanor scared her more than if he'd yelled at her. Fear spiked her temper again. "You said you don't trust me and Ben wants to breed me like cattle. You won't let me meet the other women because you're ashamed of me."

Wade took another step closer. "We *don't* trust you. You already ran off once. We told you the truth. You ain't done nothin' to earn our trust. Ben never said he wanted to breed you like cattle. He said you might already be carryin' our child, our heir. Also true, or did you forgot what we did last night?"

Tory bit her lip and took two more steps back. "No. But I said I wouldn't leave, and you don't believe me."

Wade took another step closer. "Why should we? I already told you, you ain't earned our trust. And we ain't ashamed of you. We don't trust you enough not to get one of the other women to help you run off. You even threatened it again after telling us you wouldn't do it."

Tory took another step back and panicked when she ran into the back wall. "I lost my temper. I didn't mean it. But a woman doesn't like to be compared to cattle or told she's not trusted."

Ben straightened but remained where he stood, obviously letting Wade deal with her. "I didn't compare you to cattle, and we told you the truth. We already made it plain we don't like lyin' or games, Tory. If you threaten to leave, we believe it and can't trust you. We mean what we say, Tory, and expect the same from you."

Ashamed now, Tory nodded. "You're right. I shouldn't have threatened to leave. I just have an awful temper. Sometimes I say things I don't mean."

Ben took another step closer. "What woulda happened if there was a horse saddled by the stable like last time? Would you have ridden off?"

Tory winced. "Probably."

Ben nodded. "You're too headstrong. Out here doing somethin' like that could be dangerous. It's our responsibility to teach you the dangers. You can get mad all you want. We can deal with your temper. But you can't run off doing somethin' that's gonna get you hurt. You're gonna have to learn to obey us without question. You never know when your life could depend on it."

Tory nodded. "I'm sorry. It won't happen again."

Wade nodded. "Let's make sure." He moved so fast she didn't have a chance to escape him. He lifted her effortlessly, holding her under his arm while raising her skirt.

Kicking and twisting with all her might, she couldn't get away. "What are you doing? Put me down. I said I was sorry."

With Ben's help, Wade hiked her skirt to her waist and tucked it away. "You're gonna get a spankin' for doin' somethin' you shouldn'ta done. Be still."

His calm tone scared her more than anything else. "You can't do this."

With Ben holding her legs, she couldn't kick anymore. She settled for beating on Wade's leg. "If you do this, I'll hate you!"

Wade delivered the first slap, surprising her so much she froze. "You already told us you hate us so that threat won't work."

"I didn't mean it."

Another slap landed. "You've been sayin' a lot of things you don't mean lately. We don't cotton to our wife lyin' to us, Tory."

She struggled, but hanging face down at Wade's side, she couldn't get any leverage at all. "That hurts! You can't beat me. I'm not a liar."

Wade rubbed her bottom, spreading the heat. "Nobody will ever beat you. A spankin's another thing." He ripped her pantalettes, tossing them aside and leaving her bottom bare.

"You brute. That's the only pantalettes I have."

Ben ran his hands up and down her legs. "Good. Don't wear 'em no more under your skirt."

Tory shuddered under their hands. "Let me go." Their rough hands moved gently over her thighs and bottom, holding her still at the same time.

Wade slapped her bottom again. "Are you going to throw any more water pitchers at me?"

Wriggling, she tried to kick at them again. "I already said I was sorry. Let go of me."

Wade chuckled. "Not 'til we're done. Are you gonna threaten to leave again?"

Tory gasped as a hand slid between her thighs. "I told you I'm not leaving." Another slap made her tighten her bottom. The hand between her legs distracted her into loosening up and another slap landed, one that stung even more.

Tory gasped at the heat and didn't have enough time to recover before a thick finger slid into her pussy. Surprise rendered her motionless as the finger inside her began to move.

Ben's low voice poured over her like warm honey. "You're wet again, darlin'. I think we have a wife who likes to have her fanny spanked. Not so prim and proper now, are you?"

Tory wanted to die of embarrassment. How could this kind of thing make her want to drag her husbands to the bedroom? She tried really hard to stop clenching her muscles and tightening on Ben's finger moving inside her, but she couldn't. Fighting for dignity in this position would be hard, but she had to try. "I don't like this. I'm just afraid."

Wade laughed. "You like it. You're gonna hafta stop all this lyin', darlin' or you're gonna find yourself in a heap of trouble."

"You're hurting me."

Ben stroked faster. "Another lie. You're embarrassed and aroused, but you ain't hurt."

"I am."

Ben stopped his stroking so Wade could deliver another slap. "These lies are gonna keep gettin' you into trouble."

Tory kept lifting into his strokes, unable to stop. "You brute. I hate you."

Ben laughed coldly. "I like the way you hate me. Let's see if I can make you hate me some more." He wrapped an arm around her and took her from Wade, holding her against his chest, the material of his pants rough on her warm bottom.

Tory flailed, trying to get loose. "Let go of me. What are you doing? You can't do this here. Someone could come in."

Ben placed her on her stomach over a stack of feed, shoving her skirt out of the way and placing a restraining hand on her back. "They will if you keep hollerin'."

Tory groaned when Ben's cock began to push inside her pussy, involuntarily lifting her bottom to make it easier for him. Her shock at being taken this way quickly dissipated as the overwhelming lust continued to build.

"That's good, darlin'. Push back against me. You're such a wild little thing."

Tory moaned as he filled her, tightening on him as he began stroking. "I'm, oh my, not wild or oh, not little." Her protest ended on a moan as he sunk deep and slapped her bottom again.

"You might be tall for a woman, but you're still little compared to us." He leaned over her to whisper in her ear. "And you're wilder than any of them painted ladies in the brothel. And you're all ours."

Tory kicked her legs, trying to gain purchase as he began to stroke, slow and deep. "Did you just call me a whore?"

Another sharp slap on her other bottom cheek made her burn even hotter. "No. You ain't a whore. A whore gives this to every man. This is all ours. I don't want a proper lady in my bed. I want a wildcat."

Wade ran a hand down her back and turned her to face him. "It looks like we got one. Look at how she's liftin' up." He bent to kiss her. "God, I adore you."

Ben's thrusts came faster now, going deeper in this position. "So good. My wild little wife."

Tory couldn't stop moaning. The friction of Ben moving inside her stole the last of her inhibitions. It felt so good, so good that she forgot about being in the stable, forgot about the possibility that someone could walk in, forgot everything except what he and Wade did to her.

Wade's hands stayed busy, one on her back holding her steady while the other caressed her hair. "That's it, darlin'. I love those little sounds you make."

Just as those wonderful shivers started, Ben slowed his strokes. "She's so damned tight. She's close. Hold on to her."

Tory shuddered as Wade's hand on her back firmed while Ben ran both hands over her hips and bottom. "Please, go faster."

"I will, darlin'. There's something else I wanna do first. You got her?"

Wade pushed back her hair and placed his other hand between her shoulder blades. "I've got her. Do it."

Tory got more nervous with each passing second, but found it hard to concentrate on anything other than the way Ben filled her. What would they do to her?

Ben slid his thick cock over flesh so sensitive that every stroke became as necessary for her survival as breathing.

She wanted more. She would never get enough of this.

His big hands moved over her bottom firmly and she fully expected another slap. Instead Ben's hand covered her bottom cheeks, separating them.

Frustrated that when his strokes slowed again, she tried to move, moaning her frustration when she couldn't. "Ben, I, what are you, oh God." Ben's hand lay splayed over her bottom, his thumb pushing insistently against her bottom hole.

"Relax, darlin'. Hell, she's tightenin' on my cock."

Shaken, Tory automatically fought his touch there. "You can't do that." She tightened even more, but to no avail as he continued to press. "It hurts."

"Just a little, darlin'. Let me in. I'm only gonna open you a little."

"Open me? Ben, oh!" The rush of pleasure came hard and fast as the tip of his thumb breached her tight opening. Her toes curled, her entire body tensing as Ben's thrusts began again. Hurled into almost excruciating pleasure, Tory screamed, frightened at the intensity of it.

Ben thrust hard, holding himself deep, his cock pulsing deep inside her.

Wade caressed her hair, leaning down to look at her. "Damn, darlin'."

Tory lay shaken and spent, amazed at how little she knew about her own body. Every time she thought the pleasure they gave her couldn't get any better, they proved differently. Slowly she became aware that she still gripped the feedbags beneath her and loosened her hold. Gentle hands rubbed her back and shoulders as Ben and Wade soothed her, murmuring softly to her. The scents and sounds of the horses eventually penetrated the fog that surrounded her. Tremors still ran through her that contracted her pussy on Ben's cock.

Ben's thumb still penetrated her bottom, the tip of his thumb stretching the opening. Ashamed of the way she'd responded to something so naughty, she tried to move away, only to have Wade tighten his hold on her.

"You ain't gonna pretend you didn't like that, are you?" He leaned close to brush his lips over hers, studying her face.

Ben moved his thumb, pressing a little harder. "Answer Wade."

Mortified, Tory tried to turn away, but Wade wouldn't let her. "I can't believe the things you do to me." A single tear ran down her cheek. "How could I be so bad?"

Ben withdrew his thumb and leaned over her, covering her back with his body. "We like you bad. We want you just the way you are." He nuzzled her neck, occasionally brushing kisses over her jaw. "Most men hafta go to town to get wild sex. We're lucky enough to have a woman who's full of fire. Don't try to hide your lust from us again." He straightened and withdrew slowly, running a hand over her back and bottom. "Beautiful."

Wade helped her up, pulling her against his chest for a deep kiss and sending her heart racing once again.

She could never seem to get enough of them. Leaning into him, she grabbed the front of his shirt as her knees buckled.

He lifted her against him and broke off the kiss to look down at her, his grin melting her insides. "I think I'm gonna hafta spank you more often."

Tory traced his lips. "You won't have any reason to. What about you? Don't you want to, um—?"

"Fuck?" He laughed out loud at her blush. "You are the most contrary thing. Ben can stick his thumb in your ass, but you can't cuss."

She smacked him and pushed away, both grateful and disappointed when he released her. "Stop it. I was raised proper."

Ben finished righting his clothing and patted her bottom, steering her toward the door. "That's fine. You can be proper all you want around others, but if you try to act prim in the bedroom, you're gonna get another spankin'."

Some imp inside her wanted to tease, the rare smile on his face giving her courage. She carefully schooled her features into a ladylike expression, giving him a dismissive glance as they walked out of the stable. "Sir, we are not in the bedroom and I'll thank you to keep your hands from my person."

Ben tugged her arm, bringing her to a halt. "What did you say?"

Tory laughed and broke free, running toward the house, with both men following quickly behind her. She hadn't felt so carefree in a long time. It made her giddy inside to see the surprise on the other men's faces as Wade and Ben grinned and started after her.

Right now only intimacy connected them. She just hoped she could get it to grow into something more.

Chapter Seven

Tory sat in the front room mending one of Wade's shirts. Between the two of them they seemed to have a new rip every day. They'd been married a week and gradually started to settle into a routine. She hadn't realized just how much she'd needed to have a normal life again.

With the aggression and her parent's deaths, she'd led a sad and unsettled life. On the heel of those things, her brothers' decision to head west made everyday life adventurous, but dangerous. She'd grown tired of sleeping outside, tired of riding every day. She missed sitting at a table to eat, having a warm bed to sleep in. Because of her brothers' murders, she'd moved to a strange place and married two men.

Life had been far from normal.

Looking up, she could see Ben sitting at his desk, writing in one of his countless ledgers. Wade sat in front of the desk sorting other papers, stopping occasionally to tally totals as he prepared bills of sale.

The sight of the two of them there, their low murmurs to each other as they discussed something, comforted her.

They did the same thing each evening after dinner, and she'd really come to look forward to this time of day. When they finished she knew they would join her and have a drink while they talked to her about their day or plans for the future, anything. After that they would go to bed.

Miraculously life here somehow became so *normal.* It struck her suddenly what she'd missed the most the last several months.

Security.

She felt safe now for the first time in years. She could sleep at night without keeping one eye open. Although she still sometimes had nightmares about her brothers, Ben and Wade immediately wrapped her in their warmth and talked to her, rubbing her back and arms until she fell back to sleep.

Tears stung her eyes until her vision blurred and she dropped her sewing to her lap. Security. Safety. Things she'd taken for granted her entire life and never would again.

She lived in a nice home with two men who seemed to care for her a little more each day. She didn't have to worry about shooting or cannon fire. She didn't have to look out for Indians or outlaws. She could sleep without worrying about wild animals and without ever being cold.

"What is it, darlin'?"

Tory hastily wiped her eyes, embarrassed to have been caught crying. She met Wade's eyes and smiled. "Nothing. I was just thinking about how much my life has changed since I came here."

* * * *

A possessiveness Wade usually managed to keep hidden rose to the surface, making his tone colder than he'd meant it to be. "Your life's here now. Put your mendin' away. It's time for bed."

Ignoring the startled look she gave him, he took her arm and led her up the stairs. The need to make her forget everything else built inside him with every step. She meant more to him than any woman ever had, reached something inside him he hadn't even known existed. The thought that she missed her life in Charleston scared the hell out of him.

She'd already become too important to him. He wouldn't ever allow her to leave. He couldn't. And the need to remind her just who she belonged to burned hot.

When they reached the bedroom he didn't bother closing the door, knowing Ben would soon follow. Quickly ridding her of her clothes, he lifted her into his arms, loving the way she automatically wrapped her arms and legs around him.

He lowered his mouth to hers, craving the sweet taste he knew he would find there. Knowing that another sweetness flowed even now from between her creamy thighs made his groin tighten.

Holding her softness against him, breathing in her scent, made his cock harden even more. No woman ever got to him the way Tory did.

With one hand on her curved bottom and the other in her silky hair, he bent to take her mouth with his.

God, he could eat her alive.

Her initial shyness disappeared as need took over. Possessiveness rose up again, gripping him by the throat. No one else would ever have her. No one else would be able to get past the ladylike exterior to the raw passion underneath.

The slow slide of her tongue on his aroused him even more. She lost more of the Charleston woman every day and became the temptress he and Ben both knew hid underneath.

Her soft whimper went straight to his cock, making it jump, almost bursting his buttons. He loosened his hold, cursing himself for forgetting and nearly crushing her. Her strong passion made him so hungry for her he sometimes forgot her size and delicacy.

Lifting his head, he stared down at her face. Her dazed expression excited the hell out of him. He'd never tire of seeing her this way.

Moving his hand down her smooth back, he lifted her to take a pointed, little nipple into his mouth. Her soft cries stirred his groin, tightening his balls as his body demanded release.

Lowering her to the bed, he straightened and immediately began shucking his clothes, nearly out of his mind to have her.

Her shy smile as she hurried beneath the quilt struck him like lightning. He stood there, unable to move for several long seconds as his heart nearly pounded out of his chest.

She loved him. He knew it. Why in blazes wouldn't she say it?

He reached for the quilt, throwing it to the foot of the bed. She didn't need it. He would keep her plenty warm enough.

* * * *

Tory shivered at the need on Wade's face as he threw back the quilt and reached for her. Her own need for him drove her to wrap herself around him completely as he settled over her, fisting her hands in his hair to pull him close as he lowered his head to kiss her.

He pulled her to him almost desperately, lifting her onto his lap to straddle his hips. His own desire usually flared hot and fast, but this seemed different. More.

Not knowing what caused this frantic need, she instinctively held onto him tightly trying to soothe him as her own lust soared. He broke off his kiss to lift her, his mouth closing over a nipple as he began to lower her onto his thick shaft.

"Wrap your legs around me."

Tory looked down at him in surprise. He'd never done anything like this before. Neither one of them ever put her on top. She would drop onto him and would have no way of lifting herself back off. "But if I do that—"

"I'll take you slow. I want you wide open. Do it."

His hands firmed on her bottom as she unfolded her legs and wrapped them around him. Something bothered him tonight and not knowing what made her nervous. He lowered her slowly onto his length, his face a hard mask of torment. "I can't get enough of you. You belong here. You're mine."

"And mine."

Tory's excitement grew as Ben shut the door and started throwing off clothes. "Yes. I'm yours. Oh, Wade. It's so good. How can you do this to me?"

Wade lowered her completely onto him, his grip on her bottom moving her against him. "Nobody but us'll ever have you this way."

Stunned at the hard edge in his tone, Tory rushed to reassure him. "Nobody else. I can't believe the things y'all do to me. I never imagined it would be like this."

Ben ran a hand down her back, tangling his hands in her hair to force her head back so he could nuzzle her neck. "Your accent gets thicker when you're aroused or mad. It gets my cock hard every time."

Tory's short laughed ended on a groan as Wade lowered her again. "You're not supposed to get like that when I'm mad."

Ben tightened his hold, forcing her to face him. "Like what?"

Tory tightened her hands on Wade's hair as he sucked a nipple into his mouth. "You know."

Wade scraped his teeth over her nipple and lifted her again. "Say 'your cock gets hard'."

Tory gasped as he dropped her and lifted her again. "I can't."

Ben chuckled and dropped his hand to the crease of her bottom. "I stopped on the way for some butter. I'll bet we can make you say it."

Tory couldn't even look at butter now without blushing. They'd used it repeatedly to push their fingers into her bottom, something she could never quite get used to. "No. I can't. Oh please, Wade. Faster."

Wade lowered her again, holding her pressed against him, his hands moving over her bottom until his fingers approached her tight opening. Squeezing her bottom cheeks, he made her bottom hole sting.

Amazed at the flare of lust, Tory dug her heels into the mattress to move on him as much as she could. She stilled, moaning as Ben touched a slippery finger at her stinging hole.

"Say 'I love your hard cock inside me, Wade'."

Tory opened her eyes to meet Wade's, biting her lip to hold back her cries as Ben started to push a finger into her anus.

Ben reached around her to pinch a nipple. "You know better than that. We want to hear you."

Wide open for them to do whatever they wanted, Tory knew they would make her surrender. The naughty things they did to her all the time now kept her on edge all during the day. By the time she got to the bedroom every night, her body demanded release before they even touched her.

It just got worse every day.

Tory shuddered as Ben's finger pressed into her and cried out at how strange it felt to have him enter her there. They'd done it several times but she could never get used to it. "Ben. Oh!"

Wade let go of her bottom, a hand on her lower back holding her close while his other tangled in her hair to pull her head back so he could see her face. "Tell me how good it feels to have my cock inside you."

Tory whimpered as Ben pushed his finger deep and started moving it inside her. His slow steady strokes never faltered and threatened to drive her insane. "Good. So good."

Ben chuckled and leaned over her to lightly bite her shoulder. "Let's try two fingers."

Tory squirmed, unable to stay still as Ben withdrew his finger. They turned her into someone she barely recognized with so little effort. She knew the hard, pained look on Wade's face. She'd seen it often since she'd moved in here. It told her just how much all of this churned him up. Some imp inside her fought to the surface as his cock burned inside her, each rock of her hips making her body tingle with pleasure. She licked his lips, thrilled at the tremor that went through his big body. "You like this, don't you? You're ready to come inside me."

She tightened on him and relaxed only to tighten on him again. She'd done it accidentally once and the effect had been incredible. Mocking him, she gave him a saucy grin. "Go ahead, darlin'. You know you want to."

Wade's eyes flared, exciting her even more. "You little tease. You like livin' dangerous, don'tcha?"

His harsh tone made her eager to drive him wild.

"Livin' with y'all, I have no choice." She clenched on him as hard as she could, rocking her hips as much as his hold allowed. Feeling brazen, she licked his lips again. Each time with them made her braver. They tore through her inhibitions and appeared to like it each time she let her passion loose. She'd never been able to remain proper with them anyway.

Ben cupped a breast, flicking his thumb over her nipple while pressing two fingers against her forbidden opening. "I think she's trying to make you come first. Are you gonna let her get away with that?"

"Hell no." Wade pulled her tightly against him, preventing her slight movement and tilted her head back farther, keeping her immobile to watch her eyes. "Slide two fingers into her tight little ass and let's see how much she teases me then. We'll see who comes first."

Ben ran a thumb over her nipple, sending a jolt of lightning straight to her center. "Let's get you buttered up good, darlin'."

Tory's hoarse cry sounded strange to her own ears as Ben began to press two fingers into her. Grabbing on to Wade's shoulders, she couldn't stop shaking. "It burns."

Ben continued to press against the tight ring of muscle until it gave way, allowing the tips of his fingers inside. At her startled cry, he paused. "That's it, darlin'. You're holdin' on tight, ain't you? Nice and slow, honey."

Wade's hand in her hair tightened as he pulled her close to brush her lips with his, tracing them with his tongue. "Not teasin' now, are you darlin'?"

Tory couldn't stop tightening on him, also tightening on the fingers in her bottom. Her breath came out in pants as Ben slowly worked his fingers inside her. Chills ran through her, stealing her breath as she moaned almost continuously. The low tingles, already making her squirm, suddenly became huge, taking over her body.

All at once they ran together, joining at her center and exploding. Screaming against Wade's mouth, she grabbed on to him tighter, fearing such an enormous sensation. Her cries became hoarse as it continued and her body jolted as though she'd been hit by lightning.

Wade's arms tightened around her, pulling her face against his neck as he rocked her, groaning his own release.

Ben's hand moved over her back as the tremors continued. He slowly withdrew from her bottom and bent close to speak softly to her, his lips moving over her ear. "Do you know what those sounds you make do to me?"

* * * *

Ben kissed her shoulder and moved away to the basin to wash up and to give Wade a few minutes alone with her. He needed a few minutes to settle himself before his cock exploded.

Tory loosened up a little more each day, something that both thrilled him and worried him. She seemed to become more comfortable with her life and her new home, but her growing fearlessness concerned him.

He didn't want her to be afraid of him or of Wade, but the security they'd struggled to wrap her in made her more reckless than he liked. Knowing what she'd been through, they did their best to let her know she was safe now. After two days, she stopped carrying the knives she told them had belonged to her brothers.

He'd noticed and made her carry one on her belt every time she left the house.

It hadn't done any good when she'd almost stepped on a poisonous snake while collecting flowers.

Thankfully Wade had been close by, watching out for her and shot it before it could strike. Drying his hands, he braced himself on the basin stand and fought the remembered horror of seeing Wade carrying her back to the house, his face like stone. She cried hysterically and held on to him so tightly, Ben wondered how Wade could still breathe.

Twice something frightened Tory and both times she ran to Wade. It didn't matter that he hadn't been close by either time. He couldn't help but wish he'd saved her and calmed her afterward.

Wade confessed to him later that he'd been scared to death of shooting her. She'd instinctively turned to run and Wade shouted at her to be still. She'd done it. If she hadn't, either the snake would have bit her or Wade would have hit her with a bullet.

Wade hadn't slept at all that night.

He glanced at his brother and wife wrapped together on the bed. Tory held on to Wade now as she had that day, only this time the sounds coming from her had nothing to do with fear.

Wade and Tory seemed closer than ever and although it made him happy, he couldn't help but wonder if she would trust him with her safety if she had to. Would she immediately and blindly obey him or would she hesitate?

Not trusting him could easily get her killed.

Ben looked down at his now soft cock. He knew it wouldn't stay that way for long, especially once he got anywhere near his wife.

Wade groaned. "I forgot I wanted you to say you liked my cock inside you."

Tory's giggle stirred Ben's groin. "Poor thing."

Wade narrowed his eyes and grabbed for her, wresting her to her back. "You like to tease, don't you? Is this something new you forgot to tell us about?"

Ben went to the bed, lying on his side next to them and reached out to touch Tory's arm. The tears in her eyes alarmed him. "What is it, darlin'?"

Tory turned toward him, her big blue eyes swimming. "I haven't teased anybody for a long time. When I was a little girl I used to tease my brothers all the time, before the aggression, and they went off to fight. Then nothing was funny anymore."

Ben wanted to see her smiling again. "All that's in the past, darlin'." Nudging his brother aside, he rolled on top of her, keeping his weight from crushing her by leaning on his elbows. He bent down and licked a nipple, smiling at her gasp. "Before I take you, you're going to say the word 'cock'." He leaned down to kiss her long and deep. He would never get enough of her taste.

She lifted her arms to wrap around his neck but they dropped back to the bed. Spent from her pleasure, she smiled lazily. "Never."

He sucked a nipple into his mouth before licking it with the flat of his tongue and moving to the other. He shot an amused look at his brother as Tory started to squirm. As soon as she started to get aroused, she could never lie still. It still amazed him that she thought she should.

The challenge in his wife's eyes and the way she rubbed against him made his groin tighten even more. "You will, darlin'. Your bottom's still buttered up, remember?"

* * * *

Tory wrapped her legs around his hips and lifted herself, silently urging him to take her. She knew he wanted to, his hardness pressing against her letting her know that he'd already become aroused. Still limp from the strong release a few minutes ago, she could barely move.

Wade lay next to her, brushing her hair back from her face as he watched her. "You challenged Ben now, darlin'."

Something inside Tory warmed at the way Wade smiled at her, his eyes tender as they roamed over her. It made her happy that she'd somehow calmed whatever drove him before. In their arms she felt happier than she'd been in a long time.

If only they could one day learn to love her.

Ben teased her nipple while reaching for her center, stoking the embers of the need inside her until they flamed once again.

She knew they both wanted her and liked to make love to her, but men as hard and driven as Ben and Wade would never easily love a woman.

Especially a woman who knew nothing about their way of life.

At times like this, though, both Ben and Wade seemed happy with her, and she knew that she could make them feel good. It would have to do for now.

But she just couldn't say the things they wanted her to say. "No matter what you do to me, I'm not saying that."

Ben's slow grin warned her he would do his best to change her mind. "You're going to say 'I want your cock inside me.' You're going to say it before I take you."

Tory moaned as his fingers slid through the moisture at her slit. "Just take me, Ben."

He covered her body with his, pressing her into the mattress. Lifting her hands over her head, he took her mouth with his, kissing her deeply and stealing her breath.

Tightening her legs around him, she felt his cock jump against her and shifted restlessly, trying to get it inside her, groaning in disappointment when he avoided her.

He lifted his head, smiling down at her. "Not so proper now, are you, honey? You know how good I can make you feel. You want my cock inside you?"

Tory arched, rubbing her nipples against his chest. "Yes."

Ben nipped her lip, making it sting. "Say it."

Tory couldn't get her lips around the words. Too many years of strict upbringing prevented it. "I can't."

Ben bent and took a nipple into his mouth and lightly bit it. "You will."

Stunned at the jolt of fire that shot from her nipple to her pussy, she didn't react fast enough when he lifted her into his arms and flipped her over. Wade shoved two pillows under her hips before Ben settled her onto the bed again.

With a hand on her back, Wade held her down as Ben moved between her thighs, preventing her from closing them.

Anticipating that he would slide into her the way he had that night in the stable, she lifted her bottom in invitation.

"That's a good girl. Lift up so I can butter you up a little better."

Tory squealed and struggled to get away as his butter-coated fingers touched her bottom hole. She never in her life imagined it would feel so good to be touched there. Did everyone do this?

As Wade held her in place, Ben slid two fingers deep into her bottom. When he started to stroke inside her there, she couldn't keep still or quiet.

Ben chuckled. "That's my little firebrand. Wait 'til I fuck your ass. Then we'll see if you still have that smart mouth."

Tory couldn't have heard him right. She froze, fear sending a shiver down her spine. "What did you say?"

Ben pushed his fingers deep, rubbing his cock back and forth over her clit. "You're gonna have our cocks in your ass soon. Then you're gonna learn to take us at the same time, one in each of your tight little holes."

Wade stroked her back. "Ben, I don't think she's ready for that."

Ben moved his fingers inside her, making her gasp as he continued to rub the head of his cock over her clit. "That's up to her. If she tells me she wants my cock inside her, I'll take her sweet pussy. If she won't say it, my cock goes in her ass."

Wade chuckled and kissed her shoulder. "You'd better say it or Ben's gonna fuck your ass."

Tory's body tingled as Ben kept stroking her in both places. She couldn't even think about what it would feel like to have his cock pushing into her. His two fingers stretched her so much, her bottom burned. She couldn't even imagine anything bigger. "It'll rip me in half. Please, you can't."

"Say it."

Her body shook, and she knew she would come at any moment.

Suddenly Ben stopped moving, his fingers still inside her and his cock pressed against her pussy, but he didn't move at all.

Almost mindless with need, she kicked her legs, trying to move, but Wade held her still. "Please. Do something. I can't stand it."

"Say it." Ben's low, deep tone told her he meant it.

No longer caring about anything but release, Tory turned her head. "Please, Ben. I want your c-cock inside me."

"Good girl." With that he slid deep so fast it stole her breath. With his fingers pressed deep in her bottom, it felt tighter than before.

Wade ran a hand down her back to her bottom. "Let me have her ass. That way you can hold on to her hips better."

Ben's fingers slid out of her bottom only to be quickly replaced by Wade's. "Stretch her out a little. Our darlin' wife is gonna love havin' a cock up her little bottom."

Tory's body shook uncontrollably. She would never have believed that words like those would have such a strong impact on her. With Wade's fingertips curled into her bottom opening, his other hand plucking at her nipple, and Ben fucking her pussy, she didn't stand a chance of resisting.

Everything inside her continued to build into that wonderful feeling she'd come to expect with them. She knew that when it hit her, her body would tighten on them and that it would burn. Just thinking of it excited her enough to send her over.

The quilt muffled the sound of her cry as she came. Her hoarse cries got louder until the pleasure peaked, taking her breath and silencing her scream.

Ben's thrust came hard and fast now as her sensitive inner flesh gripped him tightly.

The burn in her bottom as she closed tightly on Wade's fingers made her release last even longer. Her body jerked, the pleasure becoming so strong that it hurt.

Ben thrust deep and stilled, groaning loudly as he came.

Except for their chests heaving, nobody moved for several

minutes. Finally Wade withdrew his fingers from her bottom and ran his lips over her back. "Damn, I'm glad we found you."

Tory held her breath as Ben slipped out of her. She supposed Wade's words came as close to a declaration of love as she would ever get. "I'm glad, too."

When Ben covered her body with his, pushing her into the thick bedding, she hummed as he ran his lips over her shoulder, unable to open her eyes. "Your life is here, Tory. As long as you do what we tell you, everything'll work out just fine. And no more lies."

Almost asleep, her eyes popped open when he slapped her bottom.

Wade lifted her and placed her in the center of the bed before crawling in beside her. He pulled her close, pillowing her head on his shoulder with his arm wrapped around her. "Your other life is over, Tory. Forget it. There's no goin' back. We won't let you go now. Pretty words don't mean a thing. But we'll take good care of you."

Sensing that something bothered him, she'd been about to tell him that she loved him. His remark about pretty words not meaning anything kept her from saying it. After what happened earlier, they'd never believe her anyway.

Vowing to be the kind of woman they wanted, she sank into his warmth, murmuring her approval when Ben crawled in on the other side and snuggled against her back. She would tell them both at the right time.

They'd been right about one thing. She didn't need a gown to stay warm at night.

Chapter Eight

The next morning the men woke her up, sliding their hands over her and stealing kisses before leaving the bed.

Wade licked a nipple. "Get up, darlin'." He lit a lantern, the warm glow allowing her to enjoy the sight of their big, naked bodies as they moved around the room.

Tory sat up, not wanting to miss anything. A week ago she would have peeked at them through her lashes. Now she lay on her side and propped her head on her hand to watch everything. "What a nice way to wake up."

Ben looked up from splashing water on his face. He used to shave in the morning but now took to doing it at night. "You wanna meet the other women, don'tcha? They can answer your questions about your flowers. I'll take you out and introduce you to 'em."

Stunned, Tory could only blink at him for several seconds. Finally she scrambled out of bed. "You will? You'll let me meet them? After making Mary switch wash day I thought you'd never let me meet them."

Ben dried his face, tossed the cloth aside, and reached for a shirt. "You betray my trust one time and you won't even be let out of the house again. Hurry up, greenhorn, and get dressed. We're burnin' daylight."

Tory looked pointedly out the window. "It's still dark outside, cowboy."

Ben stopped buttoning his shirt and crooked a finger at her. "Come here." Standing with his hands on his hips, he looked every inch the rugged westerner. Even without his boots, he towered over her. The sight of him this way always thrilled her. Sometimes she just stared at him, amazed that they were married.

With a glance at Wade, who watched in amusement, she nervously started forward, wrapping the quilt around her shoulders. She never knew what Ben would do in this mood. She didn't stop until she stood directly in front of him. Keeping her eyes on his, she reached out and finished buttoning his shirt, the first time she'd ever had the courage to reach out and touch either one of them without their prompting.

His eyes flared and then narrowed. "You tryin' to tease me again?"

Her nipples hardened under his stare, brushing against the front of the quilt as she shifted. She smiled up at him coquettishly, the same smile she'd used on her beaus in Charleston. "Perhaps."

Ben raised a brow, not even glancing over when Wade chuckled. He reached inside the quilt to tweak her nipples, sending an arrow of pure need to her pussy. "If you tease me, darlin', I'm gonna tease back." He turned her and swatted her bottom. "Get dressed. Remember, no pantalettes."

Tory looked over her shoulder to find them both watching her. "I fixed the ones you ripped and made another. You'd better not rip them."

Wade grinned. "Then don't wear 'em with your skirts."

Tory went to the bowl of water Wade poured for her and started to wash up. "You two are always checking. Don't you trust me?"

Ben looked up from where he sat on the bed, putting on his socks. "I like puttin' my hands up your skirt. I don't want nothin' in my way. Hurry up." He walked out the door without a backward glance, leaving her alone with Wade.

"Why doesn't Ben like me?"

Wade paused and looked up. "What are you yammerin' about? Ben likes you just fine. Married you, didn't he?"

Tory shrugged and resumed dressing, not meeting his eyes. "Yes, but outside of, you know, he just doesn't seem to like me very much. He keeps calling me a greenhorn and telling me to stay out of trouble."

Wade sighed and ran a hand over the back of his neck. He seemed to weigh his words carefully before answering. "You're our wife, and we'll take care of you, but don't expect fancy words from us like they use back East. That way of life don't exist out here, Tory. No matter how much you miss it, there's no goin' back. You're gonna hafta settle into this one and make the best of it. You hafta learn to trust us to take care of you, Tory." He turned to walk away.

Before she could stop herself, Tory raced forward and gripped his arm. "Wade? You like me some, don't you?"

Wade pulled her close, his lips hovering over hers. "I like you just fine, darlin'."

Tory's eyes fluttered closed as his mouth took hers hard. It felt as if he tried to punish her somehow but instead of pulling away, she melted against him. The desperation he'd shown last night reappeared, making her wonder what caused it. When he lifted his head, she cupped his jaw. "What is it, Wade? What's wrong? You said you don't like lies. If you and Ben are sorry you married me, just say so. I'll go back—"

"No!" Gripping her by the shoulders, he shook her. "You're not goin' anywhere. Don't even think about tryin'."

Shaken, Tory stared up at him. "I didn't say I would leave, but I won't stay where I'm not wanted."

Wade threw her on the bed and lifted her skirt, fumbling with the buttons on his pants. Before she could even move, he thrust inside her. The look on his face scared her as he thrust repeatedly, fast and hard, into her. He looked so hard, so ruthless as he took her, nothing like the way he'd been in the past.

She held on to him, startled and wondering what made him act this way.

He held her desperately, so tightly she struggled to breathe. Burying his face in her neck, he lifted her bottom into his thrusts, holding onto her almost desperately.

It didn't take long before his big body tightened as he thrust deep and almost immediately withdrew from her. He wouldn't even look at her face as he righted his clothing. "Don't say we don't want you. We want you too damned much. But I'm not gonna be led around by the nose by a woman who threatens to leave all the time."

Tory sat up, staring at the empty doorway. *What just happened?*

She'd expected lovemaking to be like that but when compared to the way they'd taken her before, she didn't like it one bit. It made her realize just how careful and gentle they'd been with her. They'd always tried to make sure that she liked it, too.

The way Wade took her made her feel used and violated, but the tortured look on his face worried her the most. Although he'd come, he didn't look pleased about it at all.

Maybe they did care for her, and she'd been too naïve to see it.

The times she talked about leaving hurt them?

She'd considered it a matter of male pride when it might have been something more. Could she hope that they really cared for her?

With her mind racing, she started down the stairs. She had a lot to think about. She'd been so stupid! All this time they tried to show her with their bodies that they cared for her, but she hadn't known enough about intimacy to understand it.

She wouldn't say the words now. They wouldn't believe her. She would show them that she cared for them and wanted nothing more than to stay and build a future and she would do it in the only way they would believe.

With her body.

With a sense of anticipation, she headed down the stairs, only to come to an abrupt halt when she entered the kitchen. "Where's Wade?"

Ben took a sip of his coffee and shrugged. "He went out, looking madder than a hornet. You two have a fight about somethin'?"

Tory sighed and got her own coffee. "Not exactly. I asked why you didn't like me and before I knew it he got mad."

Ben set his cup on the table and sat back, crossing his arms over his chest. "Why do you think I don't like you?"

Tory started breakfast, keeping her face averted. "Because you act mad at me most of the time and keep calling me a greenhorn."

"You are a damned greenhorn and you're gonna end up gettin' yourself hurt. I already fired one man for tryin' to get in your skirts and before long I'm sure I'll have to fire others. You know nothin' about the ways out here and I don't trust you to mind me."

Tears stung Tory's eyes as she whipped around to face him. "Like I told Wade, if you don't want me here, all you have to do is say so."

"Not want you?" He stood and moved to her so fast she didn't have a chance to escape. Lifting her to her toes, he leaned over her menacingly. "I spend all day with a cock hard enough to pound nails because of you. If you even think about leavin', I'll tan your backside so hard you won't sit down for a month." Dropping her to her feet, he headed out. "I'll be back for breakfast."

* * * *

Tory listened absently as the women showed her different flowers, unable to get the events of this morning out of her mind. After she'd fixed breakfast, Ben and Wade came back in. All three of them ate in silence.

By the time they finished, Mary came in and started a running commentary on all the women she would meet. When Ben stood and told her to get ready to leave, she hurried along, eager to be on her way.

He didn't say much on the ride over, just told her a little about each woman and whom she was married to. Coming to the closest of the houses, he dismounted and helped her down. "This is my foreman, Jeb Smith's house. His wife, Lisa, will introduce you around."

A pretty, young woman came running out, her dark braid flying. "Hello, Mr. Beaumont."

Ben smiled at the woman tenderly, the way he hadn't smiled at Tory since the first time she met him. "Hello, Mrs. Smith. This is our wife, Victoria Beaumont. Would you do me a favor and introduce her to the other women? She has questions she wants to ask about flowers to be usin' in her soap."

The other woman grinned. "Of course. We all wondered when we would get to meet you. I'll be glad to help."

Ben nodded. "She's been busy learnin' her new home, and she's still in mournin'. Her brothers passed not long ago." He turned to Tory. "I'll pick you up in a couple hours. Be good."

Some imp inside her urged her to tease him, wanting desperately to see his smile before he left. Fluttering her lashes, she blinked innocently. "I always behave."

Ben's lips twitched. "Yes, ma'am, when you're not misbehavin'."

Not knowing if his smile had been for Lisa's benefit or not, she smiled back and waved him off, watching as he joined his men. She saw Wade in the distance looking her way as Ben rode up to him, but he turned away without waving.

Turning back to Lisa, she smiled warmly. "My friends call me Tory."

She spent the rest of the morning meeting the other women and learning about some of the local flowers. The other women knew quite a bit about the various plants, some she'd never seen before. She listened attentively, anxious to learn about the medicinal uses as well as which ones were poisonous.

Two flowers became of particular interest to her. The Star Lily, a fragrant white flower, would be used in her soap. She collected as many of them as she could, adding them to the basket Lisa loaned to her and promising to make soaps for the other women.

The women showed her another flower, some of the younger women giggling and blushing as they explained that they used it to prevent pregnancy. Several of the women gathered those, instructing her on how to make a tea from the leaves.

Knowing that Ben and Wade wanted her to bear their child, she stayed away from the small flowers.

Lisa approached and smiled kindly. "I'll bet those men of yours are wantin' to get you with child. Jeb and me, we've been married almost a year and nothin' yet."

Tory's face burned. "Ben keeps mentioning it and when he does, Wade looks down at my belly and smiles."

Anna, one of the older and more knowledgeable of the women, nodded and smiled. "Yep, them boys'll be in a hurry to get some young'uns runnin' around here. Be wantin' to teach 'em to ride and whatnot. My two are growed up now and work on the ranch along with my Red."

Tory laughed. "You're married to Red? He's such a nice man. Ben and Wade both seem to hold him in high regard. They told me he got his nickname because of his red hair."

Anna nodded. "Yep. He had a big mop of it that used to shine in the sun. He's a good man. Told me the shape you were in when they found ya. Pity about yer kin. But you're good now, with two men that'll take good care of ya."

Tory nodded, looking for signs of disapproval but found none. "Back home it's unheard of for a woman to have two husbands."

Anna nodded in agreement. "My sister lives back East, and she tells me the same thing. She don't cotton to the idea of more than two in a bed. But life's different out here. Not too many womenfolk and it's dangerous out here. Better ta have more than one to protect ya. Just plain makes sense. Them folks back East are more worried 'bout what's proper than what's smart."

Lisa giggled as the other women nodded their agreement. "It's 'specially nice when you got two men like yours. I'll bet your men'll keep you plenty warm this winter."

Anna laughed, a deep belly laugh that brought a smile to everyone's face and that made her ample frame shake. "That they will. I got to get back to my garden. It sure was nice meetin' ya, Tory. I'll be lookin' forward to one of them fancy-smellin' soaps. My Red'll be thinkin' he stepped into the wrong house."

Tory smiled. "I'm sorry to keep you from your chores. Thank you for all your help." The other women said their good-byes and trailed off after Anna, leaving Tory alone with Lisa. "Thank you so much for introducing me to them." She gestured to her full basket. "And for helping me with this."

Lisa hooked her arm in hers and started toward her house. "It was fun. So tell me, what's it like havin' both Ben and Wade Beaumont in your bed?"

Tory couldn't prevent a giggle, anxious to talk to another woman about it. "My mother would roll over in her grave if she knew. She told me that a woman should just lie there and let her husband do what he wanted to do. She didn't sound as though she enjoyed it. I didn't think I should."

Lisa giggled and looked around. "My mother said the same thing. But my Jeb isn't happy unless I, well, you know." Her face turned bright red, relieving Tory immensely.

"Thank God somebody else is that way. I thought there was something wrong with me."

Lisa shook her head. "I thought the same thing until Jeb explained some things to me. He said it made a happier marriage when both people enjoyed it. He said he didn't wanna share his bed with a cold woman." Lisa giggled again. "That man does things to me I've never even heard of."

Relieved and happy she'd found a friend, Tory grinned. "So it's normal?"

"I don't know if it's normal. Some of the other women here think the same way that our mothers did. A few say they like it. But I saw the way Mr. Beaumont looked at you. You can tell when a man wants a woman that way. It's nice you can make a big, strong man weak in the knees, ain't it?"

Tory shrugged. "I don't know about that. I'm still too new at this, and the two of them sometimes just overwhelm me. I don't really get a chance to do anything." Thinking about the time she'd given them release during their baths, her face burned. She wondered if she could find a way to do it again.

Lisa stopped, looking around again. "Have you taken them in your mouth yet?"

Tory's mouth dropped. "Taken their, um, you know, in my mouth? Are you puttin' me on?"

Lisa's face turned even redder. "Jeb showed me how. You just lick it and suck on it a bit. Anytime he's in a bad mood, it cheers him up real good. It also gets me out of spankin's, but I don't always want to do that."

Stunned, Tory just stared at her. "You *like* to be spanked?"

Lisa shrugged, for the first time looking uncomfortable. "Not always. Sometimes Jeb gets mad at something I've done and he spanks me for real. But most of the time it's more playful-like and…"

Tory laughed. "Oh, I'm so glad we talked about this." Not wanting her friend to feel uncomfortable, she leaned down to whisper conspiratorially. "I liked it, too. But don't ever tell anybody."

Lisa giggled again. "It'll be our secret."

Walking up the steps to Lisa's home, Tory felt like she'd found a best friend. "Would it be all right if I came out to visit you? It sure is nice having someone my age to talk to."

Lisa hugged her. "I would love that. And if you let me know when you're gonna make those fancy soaps, I'd love to help you. I can't wait to try it out. My Jeb will be all over me even more than usual."

They talked as Tory helped Lisa prepare dinner until they heard the sounds of approaching horses. Lisa wiped her hands on her apron. "That'll be my Jeb and the bosses. Jeb likes Cookie's food but he likes to come home to me for his meals. Just like your men. They used to eat in the lodge with the others until you came here."

"They did?" Tory hadn't known that. She assumed that they'd always come home to eat.

They walked out to the front porch to greet the men and Tory paid special attention to the way Jeb greeted Lisa. His eyes lit up when he saw her, crinkling at the corners as he gave her a slow smile. She'd never seen that look on Jeb's face before. Feeling like an intruder, she turned to Wade, to find a similar look on his face. It gave her hope and she smiled back, hiding her disappointment that Ben hadn't come with him.

Once they carefully loaded her assortment of flowers into his saddlebags, they started off, riding slowly across the open land. Wade put her across his lap so that she sat sideways, the way Ben did that morning.

Tory turned to watch Jeb wrap an arm around his wife and lead her into the house, leaning down to say something to her that Tory couldn't hear. Lisa giggled just as the door closed, making her smile.

What must it be like to be so confident in a husband's love?

"Did you have a good time pickin' flowers, darlin'?"

Tory nodded and kept looking straight ahead. After the way he'd been earlier that morning, she didn't know what else to do.

"I'm sorry."

Tory snapped her head up. "Why?"

Wade looked embarrassed, something she hadn't imagined possible. "I shouldn'ta taken you the way I did this morning. That's why I came out alone. I told Ben I needed to talk to you."

Tory nodded. "I'm not quite sure what to say to you. I always thought it would be like this morning." She shrugged, looking down at her hands. "I didn't really have anyone to talk to about it until today."

Wade lifted her chin. "Who did you talk to today?"

"Lisa. She's a really nice woman. I think we're going to be good friends."

Wade lifted a brow, his lips curving. "And what did you and our foreman's wife talk about?"

Tory shrugged again. "I asked her if it was all right to like it so much. She said she did, too. It made me feel better."

Wade pulled the reins, bringing the horse to a stop. "What? You thought somethin' was wrong with you because you like it?"

Tory's face burned as she nodded. "How could I know any better? My momma never told me it would be okay to like it so much. I thought only painted ladies liked it. I tried really hard not to. After what happened at the pond, I knew both of you would think badly of me. I thought that's why you decided to share me, because you thought I was like them."

Wade groaned, touching his forehead to hers. "No, darlin'. I was already crazy about you and saw that Ben felt the same way. We like havin' a woman who likes what we do in bed. We told you that."

Tory nodded. "I know what you said but liking having someone in bed isn't the same thing as caring about them. I'd hoped that maybe over time you'd see me more like a friend, like my father and mother. I thought if I helped out a little…"

Wade threw his head back and laughed. "You ain't our friend, darlin'. You're our wife. You just take care of the house and the young'uns and let us worry about the rest."

"But, Wade. I can help. I thought if I made those scented soaps I could sell them in town."

Wade started off again, still chuckling. "If you want to make those pretty-smellin' soaps, fine by me, but you don't need to sell them. Just as long as you make the regular soap. I don't wanna smell like no flowers."

Tory folded her arms across her chest. "Wade, this is not funny."

"Sure it is, honey. Now, tell me what else you and Lisa talked about."

Tory kept her arms folded and looked away, jolted when his hand slid up her skirt. "What are you doing?"

"I'm gonna make you tell me."

Tory grabbed onto him as his hand slid between her thighs, moaning when a thick finger slid into her pussy while he massaged her clit with his thumb. "Wade!"

"So what else did you and Lisa talk about? Do I have to spank you to get the truth? You don't get to come until I get my answers."

"We-hmm—we talked about that, too."

"Talked about what? Getting your bottom spanked?"

"Hmm."

"Did you tell her how much you like it?"

When she didn't answer fast enough, Wade changed the direction of his fingers.

That tight sensation grew, but he wouldn't give her what she needed to come. "Wade, please." His touch felt so good. She'd spent all day wanting to be touched after being left in such a hurry this morning. She couldn't take much more.

"Did you tell her?"

"Yes. But I'm not the only one. She likes it sometimes, too."

"Sometimes?" He concentrated on that spot once again, but kept his strokes so slow that it didn't send her over.

"Please, Wade. Faster."

"I'll do it faster and make you come real good as soon as you tell me." He turned toward the grove of trees that bordered the yard, removing his hand to hold on to her as he jumped the fence. He rode several yards until she knew they could no longer be seen by anyone on the ranch and stopped. He got off the horse and reached up for her. "Come here, darlin'. You can finish tellin' me what you and Lisa talked about."

Tory held on to him as he carried her to the base of a tree and sat, pulling her down to sit astride him.

"That's how you like to ride, ain't it, honey? Tell me how much you like havin' your bottom spanked."

Tory couldn't believe she could have this kind of conversation. "I didn't think I should like it. I thought there was something wrong with me."

Wade brushed her lips with his as he unbuttoned her shirt. "No, darlin'. Everythin' about you is just right. You're a naughty little wife, and I think you're gonna hafta be spanked quite a bit."

Tory arched, moaning as he pulled the sides of her shirt and chemise aside and covered her breasts with his hot hands. "It's really all right to like this so much?" She didn't really have a choice anyway.

"It's perfect that you like this. But only with Ben and me. We're your husbands and the only ones that got the right to touch you this way."

Tory moaned as he played with her nipples and moved on him without thinking, crying out as the rough material scraped her tender flesh.

"Easy, darlin'. We don't want to hurt that soft pussy, do we?" He tore at his fastenings until he could pull his already hard cock free. "Why don't you sit right here and tell me all about how good it feels to fuck your husbands?"

Tory wondered if she'd ever get used to her husbands' blunt language. "I've never heard anyone talk that way before."

Wade nipped her bottom lip as he lifted her and slowly lowered her onto his thick cock. "Nobody but us better ever talk to you that way."

Tory couldn't keep quiet as it filled her inch by incredible inch. Holding onto Wade's wide shoulders, she shuddered as he filled her completely.

His hands covered her breasts again. "Ride me, darlin'. You do it. Move the way it feels best."

Tory snapped her eyes open to look up at him, meeting that hooded stare that she loved so much. "You want me to do it?"

Wade's lips curved. "Yep. I'm busy right now."

Tory gasped as he tweaked her nipples.

"You like that, don't you? Let's see if you like it a little harder."

Tory squealed when he actually pinched them, the sharp pain making her tighten on the shaft inside her.

"That's it. Move, Tory. Fuck me good."

Tory would never have believed she could do something like this but the need became too strong to deny. She moved on him, taking him deep, only to lift up again. She couldn't do it hard enough or fast enough. He continued to play with her nipples, making the ache at her center even worse. After several minutes of being unable to get the right rhythm, she whimpered. "Wade, I can't do it right. Please, help me."

Wade chuckled and pulled her tightly against his chest, stilling her movements as he took her mouth with his. He easily subdued her when she struggled against him, trying to move. By the time he lifted his head and released her, she'd become wild with the need to come.

She started bucking against him, whimpering her frustration that she couldn't seem to get the right angle. She couldn't move fast enough and the hands covering her breasts distracted her. It distracted her even more when he bent to take a nipple into his mouth. "Wade. Please. I'm so close. Please. Help me."

Wade gripped her hips. "Touch yourself, Tory. Rub yourself while I'm takin' you."

She'd never touched herself this way except for bathing. Staring up at him, she didn't know what to say.

"Look at me. I want your eyes on me while you touch yourself. If you close your eyes, I'll stop."

Slightly uneasy about doing this in front of him, she didn't know what to do. She needed release badly.

Wade took her hand in his and put it over her mound. "Do it, Tory."

Tory rubbed herself as he watched. "Please. You said you'd move."

Wade's hands tightened on her hips as he began to move. "Don't stop."

Her touch didn't feel as good on her clit as his, but knowing he watched made her come. With him moving her on his length, the fluttering began quickly. Tightening on him, she came, pleasure bursting from somewhere deep inside her, quickly spreading everywhere.

Wade's strokes came faster, and he pulled her down hard, holding her tightly as he groaned his own release. He dropped his head back against the tree trunk, his neck corded as he held her firmly on top of him.

Always amazed that she could do this to him, she traced his jaw and slumped against him, burying her face in his neck. "Wade, I love you."

The hands rubbing her back stilled and Tory froze, afraid she'd said it at the wrong time. He lifted her face to his. "Say it again while you're looking at me."

Tory shrugged. "I love you. I know it's not the same for a man so I don't expect you to love me back or anything. I just wanted to tell you."

Wade took her mouth hungrily, wrapping his arms around her and pulling her close. His hand tangled in her hair, angling her head for better access as he eased back, sipping at her lips. "I never thought you'd say it. I thought you wanted your life back in Charleston. When you cried, I thought you wanted to leave."

Tory pushed against his chest to see his face. "What? You still didn't believe me? I told you I wanted to stay."

"Then why the hell were you cryin'?"

Tory smiled, tears blurring her vision. It felt strange to sit here and talk to him this way with his cock still buried inside her. "Because I realized just how much I'd missed feeling safe. During the aggression, we never knew what to expect. Soldiers arrived at our door and took all of our food. We heard shots and cannons and screams sometimes way into the night. Then Momma and Daddy got sick and my brothers went to fight. Only Will made it home in time to bury them."

Wade pushed back her hair that had come loose and smiled tenderly. "And then you left with your brothers to make a new home in a place you knew nothin' about." He stood with her and righted his clothes.

Tory nodded as she did the same. "Then those men came and killed my brothers and the coyotes came. If you and Ben hadn't come along, I don't know what would have happened to me. Sitting there mending your shirt, I realized just how long it's been since I felt safe."

Wade bent and touched his forehead to hers. "I thought you got homesick and wanted to leave."

Tory smiled, happier than she'd been in a long time. "Is that why you acted that way? Were you trying to convince me to stay?"

Wade lifted her and spun her around, grinning. "You're never gettin' away from me, darlin'."

"I'm afraid I'll hafta disagree with that."

Tory and Wade both spun toward the deep voice. Before Wade could draw his gun a shot rang out and Tory watched in horror as Wade fell to the ground beside her, blood spreading rapidly over his shirt. "Wade!"

John Dodge stepped out from behind a tree. "Your man's gone. You're mine now."

Tory fell to her knees beside Wade, hardly able to see him as tears ran down her face. "Wade, please wake up."

John grabbed her arm and pulled her to her feet, dragging her away.

Tory screamed and fought him, the pain of losing Wade unbearable. "No! What have you done? You killed him. Oh, God. You killed him." She managed to break free and ran back to Wade, covering his body with hers and hanging on to him for dear life. "Wade! Wake up. Please don't be dead." Tears ran down her face, making the image of him lying there blurry. She had to keep wiping them to see him clearly.

To her horror, his eyes remained closed as the red stain on his shirt continued to spread. Nearly hysterical, she fought John as he tried to pull her to her feet.

The rage on his face made him look more evil than ever as he backhanded her, sending her flying.

She screamed at the unbelievable pain. Her cheek and eye were on fire. She struggled again as he pulled her to her feet, but he hauled her easily over his shoulder and ran.

He threw her over the horse's neck and mounted, pulling her facedown across his lap as he raced away.

It all happened so fast she didn't have a chance to do anything. She only saw Wade lying on the ground dead. Hearing frantic voices and the sound of horses, she screamed again.

Riding this way made her nauseated. Her cheek and eye throbbed in agony, but none of that mattered anymore. Wade was dead.

She gripped Dodge's leg, afraid of falling. Just the sight of the ground rushing past made her dizzy. Everything had been wonderful and in the space of a heartbeat it all changed. She'd never see Wade again. He'd never hold her to smile at her or tease her ever again.

The sound of the horse running over the uneven ground drowned out the sounds of her sobs. She closed her eyes against the dust so she couldn't even look to see which direction they went. She could only hope that Ben would find her.

Just when she thought she would be sick, John pulled her up, catching her hair and the back of her shirt, and lifted her to sit on his lap. Pain from her hair being pulled brought even more tears. The physical pain eased but pain at losing Wade combined with fear when she realized her shirt ripped, exposing quite a bit of her chemise.

She held it together, cursing herself for not having her knife. Ben would be livid when he found out.

If he ever found her.

She'd taken it off and put it in the basket with the flowers when she and Lisa started cooking. It must be in Wade's saddlebag.

Wade. Another sob rose up in her throat and she ruthlessly pushed it down. She couldn't think about anything right now except getting away. Trying to look around John, she tried to look around him, only to have him jerk her back.

"Be still. I'm takin' you someplace we can be alone."

Tory shuddered when he squeezed her breast, wincing when he didn't let go. She tried to push his hand away but he overpowered her.

She'd underestimated him, considered him weak because she'd compared him to Ben. It struck her then just how strong her husbands, *husband*, had to be.

Poor Wade. How would she be able to live there without him?

Wade died because of her. Ben would never be able to forgive her for this.

The stench coming from John Dodge made her gag and another sob broke free when he squeezed her breast harder.

It wasn't fair. After all she'd been through, she'd found happiness despite the odds only to have it end this way.

She hadn't even told Ben that she loved him.

Chapter Nine

Ben stood by the fence waiting for Wade to bring Tory back. He'd wanted her to have a nice time today with the other women but couldn't deny that it bothered him all day that she wasn't at the main house.

He didn't know why it annoyed him so much, but he'd been antsy since he took her out to see the women. He wanted her home.

Home. Now that Tory lived here it actually felt like a home instead of a big empty house to sleep in.

The house smelled different now, intriguing scents that drew him, making him pause to breathe them in when he went inside.

The smells of a woman.

Not the women who sold their bodies in town but soft smells. He could never quite figure out what they came from but he liked them just the same. Her basket of mending sat in the front room now along with another, which held the clothing she'd begun to make for herself.

He pulled it out once out of curiosity and saw that she'd been making men's shirts. He quickly put them back, not knowing if they were supposed to be a surprise or not.

Tory turned out to be more than he could have ever hoped for. Once they made her forget her proper upbringing, she responded to everything they did with her. For some reason she saw it as wrong, but little by little she seemed to be accepting it.

She was beautiful, funny, and her smile could light up a room.

But other than in the bedroom, he didn't know how to reach her.

She looked at him warily and although he tried to be gentle and playful with her, apparently he'd failed.

Wade seemed to be the only one who could reach her.

Seeing them in the distance, he straightened. He would just have to try harder. When they veered off into the trees, he tried to squash the jealousy that rose up inside him. She belonged to Wade just as much as she belonged to him.

Ben wanted to spend some time alone with her. He hadn't really so far and he cursed himself for not taking advantage of the time he'd had with her earlier. He'd wanted to collect her afterward but Wade wanted the time alone. He'd probably wanted to talk to Tory about their disagreement earlier that Ben still knew nothing about.

Why hadn't he asked?

Shouldn't they both know what went on with her?

As soon as they finished eating, he would ask. He had a right to know, didn't he?

Waiting for them to come out of the woods turned out to be harder than he'd thought. He knew Wade would be pleasuring her, and he wanted to see her face. He wondered what she'd thought of the other women. He would bet that she and Lisa Smith would become fast friends.

He would have to tell Jeb to bring his wife over to visit. That way Tory could stay home. Before he knew it, all of the other women would be coming over.

Who'd have believed he and Wade would have ever put up with something like that?

"Whatcha smilin' 'bout, boss?"

He looked over at Shorty in surprise, completely unaware that he smiled. "Just thinking about women."

Shorty snorted. "More trouble'n they're worth, you ask me."

Ben looked toward the trees. "If you find the right one, they're worth it."

Shorty shuffled his feet. "Mrs. Beaumont's pretty as a picture. Real nice, too."

Ben narrowed his eyes. "How would you know she's nice? When did you talk to her?"

Shorty turned beet red and shuffled his feet some more. "She came out to help Miss Mary in the garden and saw me and Red and came over to thank us real polite-like for helpin' her that first night. I felt real bad about how Dodge talked to her."

"Dodge is gone and anybody else who talks that way to her will be, too."

Shorty looked up in alarm. "Oh, no, boss. I would never talk to Mrs. Beaumont like that!"

Ben smiled. "I know you won't, Shorty. But pass the word. I won't cotton to anybody speakin' with anythin' but respect to my wife."

"Yes, sir. I'll pass the word, but I think everybody already knows how you and Mr. Wade are with Mrs. Beaumont."

"Good. I want—"

The sound of a gunshot startled the hell out of him. The fact that it came from the trees where he'd seen Wade and Tory go scared him to death.

Somehow he'd mounted his horse and raced hell bent for leather toward them, his gun already in his hand. He didn't remember any of it. He heard riders behind him, but he didn't bother to turn around.

Tory's screams chilled him to the bone.

Racing to the woods, his heart pounded nearly out of his chest when it hit him just how easily he could lose them both.

He would never let Tory out of his sight again.

Please be alive. Please be alive.

He couldn't think past that.

It took him what seemed like forever to get to Sunset, Wade's stallion. His blood ran cold when he saw his brother's body lying on the ground, unmoving.

He leapt off of his horse before it even stopped and raced to his brother's side, looking around frantically for any signs of Tory. Kneeling next to Wade, he ripped open his shirt, desperate to find the source of all the blood.

Wade groaned, his eyes flickering open. "Tory."

Ben used his kerchief to wipe away enough blood to find the bullet hole. "I don't know. Where is she? What the hell happened? Who did this?"

Several of his men surrounded them. Red knelt on the other side of Wade. "Let me deal with this. You go find your woman. It's just a shoulder wound. Gonna be sore, but he won't die."

Wade groaned. "It was Dodge. Did he take Tory? Go. I'll be fine. Go get her."

Ben kept looking around, praying for a sign of her. "Looks like. Shorty, run into town and get the doc. Campbell, go find Jeb and tell him what's goin' on. Red, you're with me. I may need a tracker."

He shared a look with his brother and nodded. "I'll find her." Red stood and helped him search the ground. Ben could track with the best of them, but his oldest ranch hand was one of a kind. "He's headed south."

Red nodded and hobbled back to his horse, still limping from the trail drive. "Yep. Good for us he's in too big a hurry to cover his tracks. He'll wanna get as far away from you as he can as fast as he can. He's only got a few minutes head start."

Ben mounted his horse. "He ain't gonna make it." He started off, shouting over his shoulder, "Look after my brother."

He took off with Red and four other men. Two of them had worked for him for a while, but the other two he'd hired on for the drive. He didn't know how they would react in this situation and didn't trust them. They might be friends of Dodge leading them into an ambush.

He didn't have time to deal with it now. He could only think of getting to Tory. If that son of a bitch put his hands on her, he would take him apart bit by bit. When Red rode next to him, Ben waved the others to back off. Racing across the flatland, he could see dust up ahead.

He yelled over to Red. "We'll be on him soon. Dodge make a lot of friends?"

Red had worked for him long enough to get his meaning. "Nope. But I'll keep a watch. He ain't gonna give up. You gonna try for a shot?"

Ben immediately shook his head. "Might hit Tory." He reached back and took the bullwhip from where he kept it fastened to his saddle.

The two hands that knew him better whooped excitedly, but Ben paid no attention. He kept gaining on the bastard in front of him. Leaning over Thunder's neck, he urged him faster, leaving the others in the dust.

As he got closer, he could see that Tory's struggles slowed Dodge. He couldn't ride full out or she would fall of the horse, making everything he'd done useless. If his revenge for getting fired was taking Tory, he'd have nothing to show for it.

But killing her would also work.

If Tory fell off at this speed, she would die for sure. She probably didn't know that. Racing toward her, he saw she made it hard for Dodge to hold on to her as she fought to get free.

Jesus! If she managed to pull loose—Ben didn't even want to think about it.

Closing in on them, he saw Tory look around Dodge's shoulder and straight into his eyes. And smiled.

Smiled?

He would put her over his knee as soon as they got back home.

Thankfully she stopped struggling.

Dodge glanced back, looking panicked when he saw Ben closing in on him.

Ben knew Dodge should have heard him but probably didn't with all the noise Tory made. The evil look on Dodge's face didn't surprise him. He'd known from the beginning that the man was a few cards short of a deck and that his meanness went down to the bone, but none of that mattered on the drive. He knew he could handle him.

It mattered now. He held Tory in his arms, her life in his hands.

Ben judged his distance and ran his thumb over the handle of the whip in preparation. Adjusting his seat came naturally as he swung back and snapped his whip out, hitting the middle of Dodge's back, and ripping his shirt right down the center. He'd already anticipated his adversary's next move and cracked the whip down sharply, knocking the gun from Dodge's hand before he could pull the trigger.

Another crack and Dodge's hat came off, allowing Ben to see a little more of Tory.

Dodge's screams filled the air as the whip lashed at him over and over. Blood ran freely down his back and Ben knew it felt like fire by now.

Ben's arm stilled, horror washing over him as Dodge tried to do what Ben feared most.

Dodge tried his best to throw Tory from the horse, probably figuring that Ben would stop for her.

Ben knew he had only one shot at this and prayed he could do it. Although he'd practiced with the whip often, his aim and the amount of force he used had never been so important. If he didn't do this right, he could hurt Tory badly.

But if he did nothing, she would be killed.

The moment he dreaded had come up on him sooner than he'd expected. Tory's life depended on her trusting him blindly. Would she do it?

He knew his horse would stay straight and at a steady pace. Standing in the stirrups he blocked out everything except Tory. "Lift your arms!"

She would know if she did, there would be no way to stop her fall. Would she trust him with her life and to obey him?

Swinging the whip, adjusting the speed, he was ready when her arms lifted. Praying like never before, he lashed the whip out, just as she started to fall. The end of the whip quickly wrapped several times around her wrists and he jerked with all of his might, hoping that it held.

Thunder knew what to do and moved closer just as she flew through the air toward his legs. Dropping the handle of the whip, he caught her with both hands, yanking her in front of him to hold her tightly against his chest. "You all right?"

"Yes! Oh, God! I knew you would save me. Wade! Oh, God. He killed Wade."

Still riding fast, he chased after Dodge and yelled in her ear. "Wade's gonna make it. Gimme my whip."

The other men moved closer, Red in the lead. Ben knew his trusted hand would have kept the others back.

Tory worked the end of the whip from around her hands and pulled on it until she got to the handle. When she held it up, he grabbed it and swung it high, cracking it into Dodge's back yet again.

The other man faltered, pain obviously making him clumsy. "No more! No more!"

"Stop and I won't hit you again."

Dodge tugged the reins but pain kept him from pulling hard. "No more!"

Ben pulled Tory closer as he stopped, letting the other men handle Dodge. "Did he hurt you?"

"Wade's not dead? Really? Ben, it was awful. So much blood. Are you sure?"

"I'm sure."

"I can't believe what you did with that whip."

Ben closed Tory's shirt where it gaped in front, grimacing when he saw her cheek and eye. He carefully watched the men pull Dodge from the horse to tie him up. He held the handle of the bullwhip, running his thumb over it in preparation, waiting for a sign that one of the others would help Dodge.

Instead, they stared at him in awe. "Did you see that? Look at Dodge's back. Then he pulled her off the horse with it. Did you see that?"

Red shook his head and looked toward the seasoned hands, smiling. "We all saw that. Weren't the first time. Throw Dodge back over the saddle for the ride back."

"My back! Give me some water for my back!"

Ben looked up at the noon sun. "Oughta feel real good after riding back to the ranch on your belly. Sunburnt on top of it."

"No! You can't do this."

Tory leaned toward Dodge and would have fallen if not for Ben's quick reflexes. "You almost killed Wade. I told you you'd be sorry when Ben caught up to you."

Ben settled her back on his lap. "Damn it, Tory. Be still. You're gonna fall." It still amazed him that she'd lifted her arms with no hesitation. Fear of falling hadn't stopped her. She'd trusted him implicitly.

He felt ten feet tall and at the same time humbled by her trust.

Tory leaned against his chest. "You would never let that happen. I knew you would save me." She leaned back to look up at him. "Thank you."

Ben allowed her to pull his head down for a kiss. The second his lips touched hers, he sank into her. The aftereffects of such a close call made him rougher than he should have been, but he couldn't help it.

She was alive and in his arms, and he just wanted to devour her. Later. First he wanted to get her home and check on Wade. Lifting his head, he brushed the tangled hair back from her dirty face and ran a finger lightly over her cheek. "Did he hurt you anywhere else?"

She looked at the others, who smiled and quickly turned away, leading Dodge's horse for the ride back to the ranch. Tory pulled Ben's head down again to whisper in his ear. "He didn't hurt me much. He just kept squeezing me and now I'm a little sore."

Ben clenched his jaw. "Squeezed you where?"

Tory blushed and looked over at the others to make sure no one watched before placing a hand over her breast. "Here."

Ben coiled his whip and held it loosely as he rode close to Dodge. "Dodge, you hear me?"

"I'm sorry. I didn't mean to kill Wade."

"My brother's alive, which is the only reason you still are. But my wife has bruises."

Tory grabbed his arm. "Ben!"

"Quiet! Dodge, you listenin' to me?"

"Yes. I didn't mean to. I didn't hurt her."

Ben let the whip uncoil and drag on the ground so that Dodge could see it. "When we get back to the ranch, I'm gonna look my wife over. Before I let you go, you're gonna get another lash for every bruise I find on her."

"No!"

Ben rode ahead, aware that the new hands looked at him incredulously. When he turned to meet their stares, they quickly looked away. Good. Word would spread fast that anyone who touched Tory Beaumont would be getting more than he bargained for.

He tried to hold Tory lightly, afraid of hurting her as they headed back toward the ranch, but she plastered herself against him.

"Ben, there's something I haven't told you. Something that I didn't think I'd get to say when John Dodge took me."

Holding her close, Ben kissed her hair. "What's that, sweetheart?"

She looked up at him smiling, her face filthy, her hair tangled and wild around it. "I love you."

Ben grinned like an idiot and bent his face to hers. "That was worth rescuin' you for."

Tory punched his shoulder. "Oh! I hate you."

Ben chuckled and brushed her lips with his. "No, you don't. You love me. You just said so."

Tory looked up at him through her lashes. "Maybe I lied."

"Darlin', you already know what I'll do to you if you lie to me. Sure that's the tack you want to take?"

"You're impossible. Don't you care about me just a little?"

"You already know damned well that I do." Ben sobered, his voice low. "Tory, I don't have a lot of fancy words, and I don't speak my feelin's a lot."

"But you do love me?"

"Yep. Let's get home to Wade. He's got to be outta his mind with worry about you."

Tory snuggled up to him. "No. He'll know that you saved me. I'm worried about him. Ben, there was so much blood."

Ben inclined his head. "He'll be weak as a newborn kitten 'til he gets some back. He's gonna be a bear."

Tory grinned. "I can handle him. And you."

Ben leaned close and whispered in her ear. "We'll see if you can handle both of us just as soon as Wade's recovered."

She gasped as a shiver went though her, telling him just how much the idea excited her. Damned if he didn't love being married to her. "Well I never!"

"I know darlin', but you will."

She sputtered, her face bright red. "Wait until you see the surprise I've got for you, Ben Beaumont. You won't be so arrogant then."

"I can't wait, darlin'." He hurried back to the ranch, anxious to get to Wade, smiling every step of the way.

Chapter Ten

When they got back to the ranch, Ben carried her up the stairs despite her objections.

Mary followed behind with an armload of clean cloths. "The doctor is in with Mr. Wade. He already took the bullet out and says he'll be fine. He's stitching him up now."

Ben paused in the hallway and looked at the closed door. "That was fast."

Mary opened the door and turned. "Doc was headed for town and Shorty caught up with him. There's a bath waitin' and more hot water on for another." She disappeared through the door before either one of them could answer.

Tory struggled. "Put me down. I want to go see Wade."

"No. You can see him when Doc's through. In the meantime, I want to check you out and see where else he hurt you and if you need the doc."

He cussed a blue streak as he counted each bruise on her body. She hadn't thought he would really bring her home and strip her of every stitch of clothing, but he did. He inspected her from head to foot, his language getting worse with each bruise he found.

"Be quiet. You're going to upset Wade. Ben, you're not really going to whip Dodge again, are you?" He shot her a look and turned her, running his hands all over her. After wiping at the tears on her face, he picked up her dirty, ripped clothing and left the room, leaving her naked and unable to follow.

She sat in the bathtub, crying as she listened to Ben whip Dodge, jolting every time the whip cracked.

She covered her ears to drown out the sounds of Dodge begging for him to stop. She didn't know how long it took, but it seemed like forever. Hearing him bark out orders, she knew when it finally ended when Dodge's screams stopped, and his whimpering began.

Over the quiet, she heard Ben's voice ring out. "You're a lucky man. If my wife wasn't upstairs cryin' over me givin' you the whippin' you deserve, I'd keep goin' until you were dead."

Another silence fell and Tory sat barely breathing so she didn't miss a thing.

"I'm done with him. Dodge, you listenin'? You ever show your face around here, I'm gonna kill you. I'm gonna whip you again before I hang you. Now get off my land and don't ever set foot on it again. Any of you men see him on Beaumont land, shoot him in the leg and bring him to me."

The usual chatter coming through the window died and silence fell over the yard.

A few minutes later, Ben came back to their bedroom, his face a mask of fury until he saw her. He held her as she cried, and then carefully started to bathe her.

"Thank you for not killing him."

"Don't worry about him. He got what he deserved."

Tory rushed through the rest of her bath. "I want to see Wade."

"As soon as the doc is finished."

Tory dried off as he watched. "How many times did you hit him?"

Ben lifted her hand to kiss the bruises on her wrist and traced his finger lightly over the ones already forming on her breasts. "Eleven."

He lifted his head when the door across the hall opened. "It sounds like the doc's finished. Get dressed and you can come see Wade."

Tory dressed hurriedly and ran across the hall to Wade's room and straight to his side. "Wade? I'm sorry. I'm so sorry."

Wade's eyes fluttered open. "Why? Look at your face. Damn Dodge to hell!"

She leaned over him, wiping the tears that streamed down her face. "John Dodge shot you because of me. Are you all right? Does it hurt? Do you need anything?"

He lifted his hand toward her cheek and she quickly grasped it, holding it to her breast. "I'm glad Ben got him. 'Fraid he'd take off and I'd never see ya again."

Tory leaned down to kiss him. "Ben would never let that happen. He loves me."

Wade turned to look at Ben, who stood on the other side of the bed, before looking back at her. He smiled although his eyes kept closing. "He tell you that?"

Tory leaned down to whisper in his ear loudly enough so that Ben could overhear. "He didn't say the words but said 'yep' when I asked him if he did." She carefully crawled into the bed next to him, settling on his uninjured side. "Why did they bring you in here? Aren't you sleeping with us tonight?"

Wade put his good arm around her, dropping it heavily onto her hip. "Damned laudanum. I can't stay awake."

Ben touched his brother's other hand. "Doc said it would be better for you to sleep alone so you don't get bumped. We're gonna leave the doors open so we can hear you."

Wade forced his eyes open again. "Tell me everythin'. What happened?"

Ben eased himself onto the bed, caressing Tory's arm where it rested on Wade's stomach. "Caught up with him a coupla miles away. Didn't have much of a head start and with Tory beatin' on him, he couldn't go full out." His lips twitched as Wade chuckled. "Funny now. Wasn't so funny then. He was tryin' to hang on to her until the first crack of the whip. After a couple, the bastard tried to throw her off. Wanted to get rid of her so I would stop for her and he could take off."

Wade chuckled again and winced. "You used the bullwhip on him? And I missed it?"

Tory sat up. "Don't say that. You should have seen what Ben did to him. He hit him even more after we got home."

Wade shrugged, wincing again. "Damn it. What did Doc use, a hatchet to get the bullet out? Darlin', I'm sure Ben didn't do any more than Dodge deserved. You sure you're all right?"

Tory nodded. "Yes, I'm—"

"Besides her face, she's got quite a few bruises. Dodge decided to get a few good squeezes in before I could get to her. Her breasts and her wrists are black and blue already."

Wade tried to sit up, only to have Ben stop him. "Damn it. Let me see. That son of a bitch."

Ben nodded. "He paid for 'em. A lash of the whip for each one."

"Good."

Tory looked from one to the other. She'd gotten a firsthand look at the dangers of living in such a wild place. Montana was nothing like Charleston.

The men in Charleston couldn't compare with these men. It took hard men to live under the harsh conditions they faced every day. She listened absently as Ben continued to talk to Wade, his fingers lightly tracing the bruises on her wrist.

Relaxed now, he smiled at Wade, a sharp contrast to the way he'd looked earlier as he'd raced after Dodge.

How could men be so hard and yet so gentle?

"Come on, honey. Wade's asleep. Mary's got supper waitin' for us."

"But isn't Wade hungry?"

Ben went to the foot of the bed and held out a hand to her. "He won't be hungry 'til tomorrow. By then he'll be ready to eat an entire cow."

"But what if—"

"He'll be fine while we eat. Come on. There's somethin' I want to ask you."

They crept out, leaving the door open and started down the stairs, Ben holding her hand in his.

Tory smiled up at him, hurrying toward the kitchen. Now that he'd mentioned food, she realized how hungry she'd gotten. "What do you want to ask me?"

Ben seated her, keeping her hand in his. "Where's your knife?" His hand tightened when she would have pulled away.

"You blame me for Wade getting shot!"

Ben shook his head. "Not at all. Dodge would've shot him anyway. But you might've gotten away if you'd had your knife. We're gonna hafta talk about this a little more before bed. Eat your dinner."

Tory hid a smile at the look on his face. It looked like tonight she would have to try Lisa's way of appeasing her husband.

* * * *

Tory smiled around Ben's cock, enjoying the low groans coming from his throat. It amazed her that she could make such a big, strong man like Ben tremble under her hands this way. The feeling of power it gave her made her almost dizzy.

She released him, licking him from base to tip. "Am I doing this right?"

Ben groaned when she cupped the sack beneath. "You're doing just fine. Hell, no wonder Jeb's always smilin'."

"Maybe I should suck a little harder." She took him back in her mouth and began to suck on him harder, being extra careful with her teeth the way Lisa had warned her.

The sounds that came from Ben grew louder, thrilling her even more. Every groan, every moan increased her own excitement. Other than to help her undress, he hadn't even touched her yet. She appreciated his gentleness, especially after today, but his reaction to what she did to him now quickly changed her mind.

Drunk on power, she wanted him to feel the same excitement she did whenever he and Wade touched her.

She used her tongue, reveling in his taste as she swirled it around the tip. Looking up, she could see that he'd closed his eyes, his head thrown back against the headboard.

He must have felt her stare because he looked down, his eyes popping open and meeting hers. He held her stare as she continued to lick and suck him, his eyes hooded and dark. Lifting a hand from where he'd fisted in the bedding, he reached out to stroke her hair. "You're very good at that. Go get the butter."

Surprised Tory blinked and sat up. "Get the butter?"

Ben pulled her over him, kissing her hungrily, his hands clenching on her bottom. "If you keep that up I'm gonna come. I wanna stretch you a little more tonight. Wade'll be fine by tomorrow and we're gonna take you together. Go get the butter."

On shaky legs, Tory stood and reached for her dressing gown.

"No. Go downstairs just like that. We're alone in the house. Hurry up."

Tory grabbed one of the lamps and ran down the stairs, hurrying back with the small crock of butter they'd been using for just the bedroom. She laughed to herself when she thought about Mary's confused look when Ben told her to leave that one alone.

She ran back upstairs, pausing to look in on Wade, before hurrying back to Ben.

"Did you stop to check on Wade?"

Tory handed him the crock. "Yes, he's sleeping."

Ben smiled and tugged her arm, toppling her onto his chest. "Come here. Tomorrow night you're gonna take Wade in your mouth the way you did to me tonight. But while you do it, I'm gonna work on your bottom. Let's see how much you laugh then."

Tory giggled and snuggled closer. "I didn't laugh at you. I smiled because it felt good to make you make those noises. Did I make it up to you for not having my knife?"

Ben held her against his chest, his fingers tracing lightly over the bruises on her breasts. "No. But after what you went through today, I won't spank you. But if you ever walk out the door without carrying it again, I won't be so nice."

At times like this, Tory felt as though she walked on eggshells with him. "You're not as forgiving as Wade."

"No. I'm not."

"Wade is tough. I see the way the men look at him. But you're even worse. You scare everybody. After today, they'll all give you a wide berth."

"So?" His finger traced lightly over a nipple, distracting her.

"So I knew you would rescue me. I told Dodge he would be sorry when you caught up to him."

"He was."

"Oh, you're impossible. You need a woman to soften you up. I think you should learn how to play."

His hand slid down her body to her center. Spreading her thighs, he slid a thick finger into her pussy. "I'm playing now. And I have a woman." He took her hand and placed it over his cock. "She's not makin' me soft. In fact she's makin' me damned hard."

Tory cried out as the slick finger started moving while his thumb lightly caressed her clit. Held securely in his arms, she leaned back, arching her breasts in an invitation he readily accepted. His teeth scraped lightly over her nipple before he sucked it into his mouth.

The shock of need shot straight to her center, making her twist in his arms as she tightened on him. "Please, Ben. Take me."

His big hands, so strong, so powerful, caressed her gently. His soft chuckle as he withdrew from her excited her even more. "You said I should learn how to play. You ain't gonna stop me already, are you?" He repositioned her as though she weighed nothing, turning her over so her head rested between his knees, placing her between his splayed thighs and draping her own over them.

"Ben? What are you doing?"

"I told you. Playin'. Let's get your bottom buttered up so I can play some more."

"Oh, God." Tory grabbed on to the quilt, shivering. Her legs bent because of the headboard, her knees on either side of his hips. With her bottom lifted over his thighs, it spread her wide, leaving her vulnerable in a way she had never been before.

He lifted her again, positioning his thick heat against her pussy, pulling her back onto it. "Now you keep busy while I play."

Thrilled that his cock now filled her, Tory groaned her frustration when he didn't move. "Ben, please!" She shivered when a slick finger pushed at her bottom hole.

"Please what?"

"Please move!"

"I've got to stretch you a little back here for tomorrow night, when I fuck your tight little bottom. You want to move, you go right ahead."

"You're mean."

"Yep. You think I'm mean now, wait 'til I get my cock up your ass."

Tory started moving, unable to wait any longer. Using her hands and knees, she rocked her body onto him over and over. She could take him as fast or slowly as she wanted and as deep or shallowly as she wanted as well.

After a few strokes, she forgot about what it must look like to him to have her bottom bucking practically in his face. He could see everything.

But it felt too good to stop.

Getting her rhythm, she moved faster and faster, taking him as deeply as she could with each stroke. The finger poised at her bottom hole pushed into her and she found herself taking more of it on each stroke.

It felt so incredibly naughty to have something invade her bottom hole and even naughtier to know that he watched it.

"You like this, don't you, darlin'? Look at you, fucking my cock and finger into you."

Shivers raced through her when he added another finger, stretching her opening even wider. Slowing her strokes, she struggled to adjust, her hoarse cries filling the room. "Ben, I can't do it. Help me."

"I'm gonna spread you good, Tory." He withdrew his fingers so abruptly it left her bottom hole clenching at emptiness.

She started moving faster, each stroke rubbing his manhood against something inside her that had her climbing. She shrieked, trembling when he grabbed her bottom cheeks in each of his hands, pushing two thumbs against her tight opening. "Ben, you can't."

"It's gonna hafta stretch to take my cock, Tory. Loosen up." His low, deep tone sounded even rougher than usual. His harsh playfulness scared her, but it also excited her.

Tory buried her face in the quilt to muffle the sounds she made as he worked his thumbs into her and began to spread her. Gripping her tightly, he moved her on his cock, spreading her bottom hole even more.

She shrieked at the slight pain but at the same time she found herself aiding his thrusts, needing more of him inside her. Her release loomed close, and she would do anything to have it. The thumbs inside her woke sensations in her she couldn't understand.

"That's my girl. Fuck me, darlin'. Let me spread you just a little more."

She would swear she could feel air touching her where his thumbs parted her, something that made her even wilder. She belonged to him. At that moment he could do whatever he wanted with her.

Giving herself over to the overwhelming surrender, she screamed as her release washed over her.

Ben's groans as he pumped into her told her how good this felt to him, too. His hands tightened on her even more. "This ass is mine tomorrow night."

Tory just started to come down when Ben pushed deep, holding her to him as he pulsed his seed into her. Collapsing on the bed, she moaned, smiling as the hands that held her so firmly now began to caress her. A slap on her bottom made her jump.

"Next time, don't forget the knife."

Tory slid off of him and turned to kneel between his thighs, leaning in to touch her lips to his. "If that was to punish me, you failed."

Ben leaned forward to take a nipple between his teeth, closing them threateningly and drawing a sharp gasp from her. Sitting back, he smiled arrogantly. "When I punish you, darlin', you'll know it."

Chapter Eleven

Tory woke when Wade snuggled against her. Immediately wide-awake, she sat up and reached for him. "What's wrong? Are you all right? Do you need the doctor?"

Wade laughed softly and rolled her to her back. "Nope. I need a kiss, a cuddle, and breakfast."

Ben groaned and sat up, kissing her shoulder before he got out of bed. "I told you he'd be hungry this mornin'. Mary's already got breakfast cookin'." He lit one of the lanterns and pulled the sheet aside to inspect the bruises on her breasts.

Wade whistled. "Damn. That son of a bitch."

Tory leaned into Wade, careful of his shoulder. "It doesn't hurt unless I press on it. He got far worse than I did. I think Ben scared the bejesus out of a lot of your hands yesterday."

Wade looked up at Ben questioningly.

Ben shrugged as he reached for his pants. "A coupla the new ones."

Wade chuckled. "The ones that ain't never seen you use the whip." He lifted Tory's chin, brushing his lips over hers. "I'm sorry I didn't protect you yesterday. If you'd been with Ben, that never would have happened."

Both Tory and Ben spoke at once.

"Bullshit!"

"No!"

Tory jumped at Ben's tone and cupped Wade's jaw. "Wade, you can't blame yourself for what John Dodge did. You got hurt because of me. If I hadn't been so rude to him, he might not have done it."

Both men scowled at her. Ben shook his head. "You two can blame yourselves 'til the cows come home, but Dodge is the one who's at fault. I'm goin' down to eat."

Tory watched him go and turned to Wade. "You wouldn't believe what he did to save me. He used the whip to pull me onto his horse. I still don't know how he did it."

"Ben's tough, Tory. Probably the hardest man I've ever met. But when he loves somebody, he loves them with everythin' he's got. He was willin' to give you up for me. That's why he stayed away from you after that night at the pond. Not because he didn't like you, but because he likes you too much."

"He *does* love me, too, doesn't he?"

Wade smiled and kissed her nose. "He does. He told me that he really didn't know if he would be able to go through with givin' you up. Now that he married you and has taken you, he'll do whatever it takes to make you happy. Just don't expect fancy words from him, Tory. Just because he doesn't say it, don't mean he don't feel it."

* * * *

Ben smiled, turning away from the doorway and started down the stairs. Thank God Wade had the tongue for the things he couldn't voice. He would have to say the words at some point, he knew, but not until he got a little more comfortable with them.

It lightened the weight on his shoulders to know that she trusted him. Her absolute faith that he would rescue her still astounded him. He'd never forget the look on her face as she smiled at him over Dodge's shoulder and the way she'd left herself vulnerable by putting her hands in the air and trusting that he would catch her.

If he'd missed—

No, he couldn't think about that. He hadn't missed, and she lay safe in his bed even now.

He would have to keep up with his practice with the whip. Who knew when he would ever need it again?

He found himself smiling several times over breakfast as Tory looked at him shyly and blushed. How she could still blush after all they'd done to her, he didn't know, but he couldn't deny that his cock stirred every time she looked at him with that shy smile and her face turned that adorable shade of pink.

It reminded him of the way she'd looked at Wade that day and it melted something inside him he hadn't known had been frozen. Remembering how she'd trusted him with her body last night made his cock stir to life.

Just for the hell of it, he reached for the butter, offering it to her. "Here, darlin'. I know how much you like havin' your biscuits buttered."

Wade choked on his coffee and to Ben's great amusement, Tory turned even redder.

Narrowing her eyes at him, she gave him what he thought of as her schoolmarm look. "You're just plain mean, Ben Beaumont."

"And you're so easy to fluster, Victoria Beaumont."

When she stuck out her tongue at him, he laughed harder than he'd laughed in years.

* * * *

Tory couldn't stand it. She'd already pricked her finger about a dozen times as she worked on her mending, her nerves frayed as she waited for Ben and Wade to finish their ledgers. The way Ben kept looking up at her and smirking, she knew he knew what went on inside her.

He finally leaned back and stretched, pulling his shirt tightly across his muscled chest. "How you feelin', Wade?"

"I'm fine. Quit askin' me that. I swear, you and Tory are a pain in my backside."

Ben lifted a brow. "I just wanted to know because Tory has a surprise for you tonight. Wanted to see if you're up to it."

Wade spun in his chair. "Really? What kind of surprise?"

"She learned a little about suckin' cock from Lisa and needs the practice."

Wade's eyes widened and he shifted in his seat. "Holy hell!"

Tory's face burned at Ben's language. She knew he did it to rattle her. "Ben Beaumont!"

He leaned back in his chair, smiling faintly. "Since your shoulder's out of commission, she's gonna ride you while I fuck her ass."

If possible, her face burned even hotter. "You are so crude, Ben Beaumont."

"And I'll bet your pussy's already wet, Tory Beaumont."

Wade looked at her incredulously. "What the hell did you two do while I was knocked out last night?"

Ben shrugged. "Tory said I needed to learn how to play."

"Did she? Did you play?"

"I did."

Wade turned back to her. "Did Ben play good?"

Tory squirmed in her seat. Already aroused, she didn't need their reminders of what Ben did to her the night before. "He's learning."

Wade threw his head back and laughed as Ben stood and strode toward her.

"Learnin', am I? Why don't we show Wade just how wet you are thinkin' about how I played with you last night?"

As soon as he reached her, he tossed her mending aside and picked her up, lifting her dressing gown as he wrapped her legs around his hips. He kissed her deeply as he moved to stand in front of his brother.

They'd already bathed and Ben made her wear just her dressing gown to come downstairs. She wore nothing beneath it. Because of that, nothing stood in the way of Wade sliding his fingers through her moisture.

"You're right. She's awful wet. Kinda like that night at the pond."

Tory broke off the kiss to glare over her shoulder at Wade. "Stop talking about that night. It meant nothing to you."

Ben nuzzled her neck. "I'll never forget that night as long as I live."

"You made fun of me."

"Did I?"

"You know you did, you bully. You made me feel things I never felt before and then, well, you know what you did and told me to stay away from Dodge."

"What did I do?"

"You know."

Wade slid a finger inside her. "What did he do?"

Tory leaned against Ben, closing her eyes as Wade began to stroke her pussy. "He licked his fingers."

Ben chuckled in her ear. "Couldn't help it. I was dyin' for a taste. My cock was so hard, holdin' on to you while you wiggled and made all them noises. Kinda like now."

Wade came to his feet behind her, still stroking her intimately. "All wet and wiggly."

Tory gasped as he ran a finger over her clit. "You made fun of me. It meant nothing to you."

Ben's lips touched her ear. "Married you, didn't we?"

Tory shuddered as Wade's hand covered her breast. "Oh! I hate both of you."

Ben lightly bit her earlobe. "There's that lyin' again."

Wade leaned in to touch his lips to hers. "Gonna hafta do somethin' 'bout that."

Ben nuzzled her neck again, making her shiver. "She can make it up to us upstairs." He turned, pulling her from Wade's touch and carrying her up the stairs.

Wade followed. "Hey, I ain't done yet."

Ben shot a glance over his shoulder. "We're just gettin' started."

Tory giggled as Ben practically ran up the stairs. "Are you in a hurry?"

Ben playfully nuzzled her, something that both touched and surprised her. He didn't play often, but when he did, it made it an event. "I'm always in a hurry to get inside you, darlin'. Knowing that I'm gonna be takin' that tight little ass of yours kept me hard all day."

Cupping his jaw, she turned his face toward her, need already making her tremble. "Ben, I'm scared. I don't know if I can do this."

Ben rubbed her nose with his. "By the time I'm ready to take you there, you're gonna want it. If you don't, we'll stop. We're not gonna do anything that you don't like. You're gonna squeal and make all those sounds that make us crazy."

Wiggling against him, Tory leaned back to give him better access as his hand covered a breast. "Awfully sure of yourself, aren't you?"

Ben set her on her feet and untied her gown, pushing it off her shoulders to let it puddle on the floor. "I'm awful sure of you. I'm gonna go get the butter. Be a good girl and help Wade get into bed."

Wade came into the room, carrying the small crock. "No need. I stopped for the butter."

Tory groaned as Ben bent to kiss her nipples. "I have a hard time eating butter any more. Mary said something today about how much butter y'all seemed to be using lately."

Wade laughed, handing the crock to Ben, and started unbuttoning his shirt. "We'll have to make sure to put in a good supply."

Tory slid her hands over his chest, unable to keep from staring at the bandage on his shoulder. She touched it gently and stood on her toes to brush her lips over it. "Are you sure you feel good enough for this?"

Wade ran his hands over her breasts. "When you get that mouth on me, darlin', I'll be good enough for anythin'."

Laughing, she took his shirt from him and threw it toward a chair. She'd never known that laughter could go with intimacy. It felt really good. "Ben taught me how to do it right. He was very patient."

Wade kicked his pants away. "Yeah, I'm sure it was a real hardship for him." He got into bed, wincing slightly as he stretched out. "Come here and show me what you learned."

Tory snuck a glance at Ben who stood naked next to the bed, his hand slowly moving up and down the length of his cock. Gulping, she eyed him warily. "Ben, I don't think this is possible."

His grin weakened her knees. "You're gonna love it, darlin', I promise. Remember, I won't do anythin' you don't like. Now get up there and show Wade how good you are with that mouth."

Tory sent him one of the saucy smiles she knew he liked and crawled into the bed, settling herself between Wade's feet. Her body already hummed and the look on Wade's face just excited her more.

With his eyes half-closed, he watched her get into position. He didn't look as composed as he usually did, all playfulness gone. His thighs tensed under her hands and he actually jolted when she touched his cock.

The feeling of power it gave her sent her pulse racing. But the surge of love added even more, nearly overwhelming her. She smiled at him tremulously. "I almost lost you yesterday. I love you so much. Let me show you."

Wade's eyes flared and his muscled body tightened beneath her hands even more.

Deciding to go slowly, she lowered her head and licked him from base to tip. Smiling when he lifted his hips, she did it again. And again.

"You're killing me."

Tory smiled mischievously. "You don't like it?"

Wade narrowed his eyes even more. "I'm hurt. You're supposed to take care of me."

Tory took him into her mouth as far as possible and sucked as she drew her mouth down to the tip, smiling around her mouthful as he groaned. Licking the tip, she ran her tongue under the underside in the way that drew groans from Ben. Lifting her head, she raised a brow. "You said that you're fine. You've been yelling all day about Ben and me coddling you."

"Tory Beaumont!"

Cupping his sack, she licked him again. She loved playing this way and some imp inside her wanted to see how far she could go. "Yes, Wade Beaumont?" Taking him as deeply as she could, she began sucking.

Whatever he'd wanted to say came out in groans and curses so garbled she didn't understand a word of it.

Ben sat beside her and ran a hand down her back. "I think you've made Wade speechless, darlin'. Let's see if I can do the same to you."

Tory moaned as Ben moved in behind her and brought her to her knees over Wade. The sounds coming from Wade urged her on and she sucked harder. Earning even more deep groans sent her own excitement higher, as did Ben's touch as he spread her thighs wide and began to stroke her slit.

"Wet already. Wade and I are lucky men to have a wife who gets wet so fast."

With his good arm, Wade slid his fingers into Tory's hair. "And one who does things like this. She's damned good with that mouth. Slow down, honey. I wanna come in your pussy, not your mouth."

Ben leaned over Tory's back and kissed her shoulder, sliding a finger inside her. "It's all nice and wet for you. Now I'm gonna butter up her bottom. You ready, darlin'? You ready to have both of us inside you?"

Tory moaned around Wade's shaft and arched her hips higher. She couldn't keep still as Ben's finger slid out of her and began to play with her clit. The touch of his cock against her leg made her shake with excitement. Those wonderful sensations began gathering again, her body tightening more and more with every stroke of his rough finger. When he stopped, she whimpered, twisting her hips as she tried to follow him.

Ben ran a hand over her bottom. "Easy, darlin'. I don't want you comin' yet."

Groaning her frustration, she continued to use her mouth on Wade until he tightened his hand in her hair and pulled her away. "Enough. No more. Ben, help her get on top of me."

Ben touched a buttered finger to Tory's bottom hole, making her shudder. "Let me get her buttered up first."

Tory fisted her hands in the bedding, her face against Wade's belly as Ben started to push a finger into her. It slid in easier than before, allowing him to immediately push it deep. Groaning, she tried her best to stay still as he withdrew it, only to press against her opening with two fingers.

Even though she'd expected it, the slight sting as he opened her a little more startled her. Every time he entered her there it took over something inside her, making her feel incredibly vulnerable. The firm hands holding her reminded her again of their strength, increasing the sense of helplessness.

Her trust in both of them, though, allowed her to revel in their masculinity, knowing that they would never hurt her. Knowing a word from her would stop both of them allowed her to let herself go and follow wherever they led.

What they wanted to do to her now scared her a little, but she couldn't wait to have both of the men she loved inside her. She found herself loosening more with each of Ben's strokes, her cries getting louder as he stretched her.

A hard arm wrapped around her waist from behind, lifting her. Ben's lips touched her ear. "Now, darlin'. We're both gonna have you."

Tory trembled uncontrollably as Wade poised the tip of his shaft at her opening and Ben lowered her onto it. Her body automatically started gripping him as he entered her, her need for release getting closer. Full with her husband, she fisted her hands on his chest and started moving.

Carefully moving his shoulder, Wade held on to her, groaning. "No, honey. Stay still. Ben and I'll do all the work."

Tory whimpered in frustration. "I can't stay still. It feels too good."

Ben kissed her shoulder and pressed his hand on her back to lower her onto Wade's chest. "It's gonna feel even better, darlin'. Wade, can you hold her?"

Wade's good arm tightened around her. "I got her."

Tory buried her face in his neck. "Why are you holding me so tightly? Oh!" The reality of having Ben's shaft press at her tight opening didn't feel like what she'd expected. Startled at the insistent press of the tip pushing into her, the pinch and burn of it made her jolt.

Wade turned his face to kiss her hair, his voice ragged. "You're gonna try to buck him off, honey. Nice and easy."

Chills went through her as Ben pushed against her tight opening, a hard hand on her back helping Wade hold her down. Tory whimpered against Wade's good shoulder as the tight ring of muscle gave way. Impossibly stretched, Tory couldn't believe she had both men inside her. Pants, whimpers, and moans spilled out of her continuously. "I'm so full. Holy juniper, it feels like you're everywhere."

Wade's fingers clenched on her back as he groaned. "So tight. Hell."

Ben's voice sounded as though he'd swallowed shards of glass. "Hold on to her. Don't you dare move. I've only got the head inside her."

Tory whimpered. "There's more? Ben, I can't." She gripped Wade tighter as Ben moved, pushing a little more of his length into her bottom before withdrawing a little. She didn't have time to do more than drag in a shaky breath before he pushed back again.

Both men held on to her, the sounds coming from them sounding as tortured as her own. Ben continued to work his thick cock inside her, each slow stroke taking him a little deeper.

The place between her legs burned. Her clit throbbed continuously, but she couldn't move enough to work herself on Wade's hard body and get the friction it demanded. Taken as never before, Tory couldn't stop clenching on both of them. "Too full. Too much." Being taken so completely shocked her into immobility. The intimate stretching overwhelmed her more than she could have imagined.

Ben's voice was barely recognizable. "A little more. Almost have it all. So tight. Ahh! I'm in."

Tory would never have dreamed that her body could stretch this way.

Both loosened their grips, caressing her as they murmured softly to her, their voices so low and deep it thrilled her, knowing that they found pleasure in her.

Wade helped her sit up slightly, running his hands over her breasts.

Throwing her head back, she cried out repeatedly, unable to stop. Full to bursting, her body shuddered as they began to move, their slow, steady strokes robbing her of all thought. With her hands fisted once again on Wade's chest, she held on as they moved in and out of her, each thrust of their shafts sliding over delicate flesh and wringing moans from deep inside her.

She could feel every single bump and ridge of their intimate caresses, the extreme fullness causing hot tingles to race through her.

Wade felt even bigger inside her, stretching her and making her pussy burn. Ben's cock inside her ass burned incredibly, creating sensations she'd never experienced before. Her ass felt so full, it seemed impossible that he didn't rip her apart, but at the same time she wanted more. Ben's cock moved over flesh so incredibly sensitive, she couldn't stand it.

Ben held her hips still as his strokes increased in speed. Wade's hands moved over her breasts lightly, even now careful of her bruises. His fingers teased her mercilessly, moving closer and closer to her aching nipples.

She felt them everywhere, all at once, and her mind couldn't take it in fast enough. With her husbands surrounding her with their heat and strength, their thick shafts moving relentlessly inside her, she became completely theirs, losing herself to their demands. The level of intimacy stunned her and turned her into nothing more than a creature of need.

She didn't care about anything now except the pleasure, her senses heightened to an awareness previously unknown to her. Taken as never before, she surrendered to it as her body clenched demandingly on both of them. The heat in her bottom threatened to consume her. The combination of both of them, pressing sure and strong into her, forging their way deep inside her took her over completely.

She couldn't think, she could barely breathe, crying out with each forceful thrust.

The tingles came stronger now, her body overloaded with sensation. As Wade's thumbs abraded her tender nipples, it all became too much to bear. With a startled cry, she went over, involuntarily gripping both of them tighter.

Both men cried out hoarsely, their strokes going deep. Ben's grip tightened as he leaned over her, growling his release in her ear as her pussy and ass tingled and tightened a sensation so strong it touched every inch of her body. Wade soon followed, surging upward into her, his hands closing over her thighs.

Tory couldn't get enough air in her lungs and would have fallen forward if not for Ben's hold.

Burying his face in her neck, he growled roughly. "I love you, Victoria Beaumont."

* * * *

Lying between them afterward, Tory smiled against Ben's shoulder. Her body still trembled, tingling in the aftermath of something so strong she wondered if she'd ever recover.

Both men touched her, their hands moving gently over her as she started to slide into sleep. Drowsily she whispered, "I'm so glad we did that. I didn't think I'd be able to handle it. Thank you for being so patient with me."

Wade kissed her shoulder. "We love you. Thank you for trusting us."

His low, sleepy whisper made her smile. "I'm just glad there are no surprises. Now I've done it all."

Ben's laughter rumbled in his chest. "What makes you think you've done it all? We haven't even tied you up yet."

Wade slid a hand over her bottom. "Or spanked you while we fucked you."

"Or had you suck cock while you're being fucked."

"Or fucked you on a horse."

"Or made you sit with a cock in your ass."

"Or fucked you on the table."

"Or eaten your pussy while you're naked on the table."

"Or draped you over the back of a chair and fucked you from behind."

"Or—"

"Stop!" Tory hid her face in the pillow as images of each scenario flashed through her mind. Even though she'd just had such an enormous release she still trembled, their suggestive comments had her body stirring again.

Amazed, she lifted her head to look at each of them, to find them watching her with lazy smiles. "You want to do all those things to me?"

Wade grinned. "And more. You didn't let us finish."

Ben chuckled. "I don't think we'll ever finish. I keep gettin' new ideas. I think we'll take a ride one day back to the pond."

Tory dropped her head back onto the pillow. "Oh, God."

Wade turned her to her back and slid a finger into her still slick center. "You wear the Beaumont brand now, darlin'. There's no escapin'. We love you too much to let you go."

Tory gripped Ben's shoulder as he leaned over her. She cupped Wade's jaw, smiling even as she spread her thighs wider for his attention. "I have no plans to escape. I have everything I want right here."

Ben slid a hand down her body to the throbbing nub at her center. "So do we, Victoria Beaumont. Even more than we hoped for."

Tory arched into their caresses, already racing to come. Their actions spoke louder than any pretty words, but the words they did use melted her heart. Looking at each of them, she smiled, knowing she was loved in a way she'd never find anywhere else. "Show me."

THE END

Siren Publishing, Inc.
www.SirenPublishing.com

Lightning Source UK Ltd.
Milton Keynes UK
29 July 2010

157589UK00008B/90/P